ILLUSTRATED TALES FROM
SHAKESPEARE

ILLUSTRATED TALES FROM
SHAKESPEARE

A MODERN ADAPTATION FROM THE CHARLES AND MARY LAMB CLASSIC

SUNBURST BOOKS

This title published 1993 by Sunburst Books, Deacon House,
65 Old Church Street, London SW3 5BS

Reprinted 1994 (twice)

© 1992 Aventinum, Prague

Illustrations by Karel Toman
Graphic design by Aleš Krejča

ISBN 1 85778 021 3

Printed in Slovakia
1/99/43/51-04

300490497

Contents

The Tempest

There was an island in the sea; its only inhabitants were an old man, called Prospero, and his daughter Miranda, a very beautiful young woman. She had come to this island so young that she had no memory of having seen any human face other than her father's.

They lived in a cave made out of a rock; it was divided into several rooms, one of which Prospero called his study. He kept his books there. These were chiefly books of magic, popular among all learned men at that time. A knowledge of magic had proved very useful to him, for this island, where he had been thrown by chance, had been enchanted by a witch called Sycorax, who died there a short time before his arrival. Prospero, through his skill as a magician, released many good spirits that Sycorax had imprisoned inside large trees, because they had refused to do her wicked commands. These gentle spirits were obedient to Prospero ever afterwards. Ariel was the chief of these spirits.

The lively little sprite Ariel had nothing mischievous in his nature, except that he took rather too much pleasure in tormenting an ugly monster called Caliban. After all, he owed Caliban a grudge because he was the son of his old enemy Sycorax. Prospero had found Caliban in the woods — a strange misshapen thing, more ape than human. He took him home and taught him to speak. Prospero would have been very kind to him, but the evil nature which Caliban had inherited from his mother Sycorax would not let him learn anything good or useful. Therefore, he was employed as a slave to fetch wood and to do the most laborious work, and Ariel had charge of him.

When Caliban was lazy and neglected his work, Ariel, who could make himself invisible to all eyes but Prospero's, would pinch him slyly and sometimes push him into the mud. Then Ariel, looking like an ape, would make faces at him. Then, swiftly changing his shape to look like a hedgehog, he would lie in Caliban's way. Caliban feared the hedgehog's sharp quills would prick his bare feet. Whenever Caliban neglected the work Prospero had commanded him to do, Ariel would torment him with these sorts of irritating tricks.

As he could control these powerful spirits, Prospero could use them to command the winds and the waves of the sea. At his orders they raised a violent storm, in the middle of which, struggling with the wild sea waves that every moment threatened to swallow it up, he showed his daughter a fine large ship. He told her that it was full of people like themselves. 'O my dear father,' she said, 'if by your magic you have raised this dreadful storm, have pity on their terrible distress. Look! the vessel will be smashed to pieces. Poor souls! they will all die. If I had the power, I would sink the sea beneath the earth rather than let the good ship be destroyed with all the precious people in it.'

'Don't worry, Miranda,' said Prospero, 'no harm is done; I have arranged things so that no person in the ship will be hurt. What I have done has been to care for you, my dear child. You are ignorant of who you are or where you came from. You know nothing more about me except that I am your father and live in this poor cave. Can you remember a time before you came here? I don't think you can, for you were not then three years old.'

'Certainly I can, sir,' replied Miranda.

'What?' asked Prospero; 'another house or something else? Tell me what you can remember, my child.'

Miranda said, 'It seems to me like remembering a dream. But didn't I once have four or five women who looked after me?'

Prospero answered, 'You had, and more. How is it that this still stays in your mind? Do you remember how you came here?'

'No, sir,' said Miranda, 'I remember nothing more!'

'Twelve years ago, Miranda,' continued Prospero, 'I was the Duke of Milan and you were a princess and my only heir. I had a younger brother. His name was Antonio and I trusted everything to him. As I was fond of quiet and deep study, I usually left the management of my state affairs to your uncle, my false brother (for so, indeed, he proved). I neglected all everyday business, buried myself in my books and spent my time improving my mind. My brother Antonio, being in possession of my authority, began to think he was the duke. The opportunity I gave him of making himself popular among my subjects aroused in his bad nature a proud ambition to steal my dukedom. With the assistance of the King of Naples, a powerful prince, who was my enemy, he soon succeeded in doing this.'

'Why didn't they kill us then?' asked Miranda.

'My child,' answered her father, 'they didn't dare; my people loved me too much. Antonio carried us on board a ship, and when we were some way out at sea, he forced us into a small boat, without either tackle, sail, or mast. He left us there, as he thought, to die. But a kind lord of my court, called Gonzalo, who loved me, had secretly placed water, food, clothes and some books which I prize above my dukedom in the boat.'

'O father,' said Miranda, 'what a nuisance I must have been to you then!'

'No, my love,' said Prospero, 'you were a little cherub that saved me. Your innocent smiles made me bear up against my misfortunes. Our food lasted till we landed on this desert island, since when my greatest pleasure has been in teaching you, Miranda, and you have done well by my instructions.'

'Heaven thank you, dear father,' said Miranda. 'Now please tell me, sir, your reason for raising this sea storm?'

'Know, then,' said her father, 'that by means of this storm, my enemies, the King of Naples and my cruel brother, are thrown ashore on this island.'

When he had finished speaking, Prospero gently touched his daugther with his magic wand and she fell fast asleep. The spirit of Ariel just then presented himself before his master to say what had happened during the tempest and where he had put the ship's company. Although the spirits were always invisible to Miranda, Prospero did not want her to hear him talking to the empty air, as would seem to her.

'Well, my brave spirit,' said Prospero to Ariel, 'how did you get on?'

Ariel gave a little description of the storm and of the terrors of the sailors. He told how the king's son, Ferdinand, was the first one to leap into the sea and how his father thought he saw his dear son swallowed up by the waves and lost.

'But he is safe,' said Ariel, 'in a corner of the island, sitting with his arms folded, sad about the loss of the king his father, whom he believes drowned. Not a hair of his head is injured and his princely clothes, though drenched in seawater, look even fresher than before.'

'That's my clever Ariel,' said Prospero. 'Bring him here. My daughter must see this young prince. Where are the king and my brother?'

'I left them,' answered Ariel, 'searching for Ferdinand, whom they have little hope of finding, thinking they saw him die. Of the ship's crew, not one is missing, though each one thinks himself the only one saved. The ship, though invisible to them, is safe in the harbour.'

'Ariel,' said Prospero, 'you have done your job well, but there is more work yet.'

'Is there still more work?' asked Ariel. 'Let me remind you, master, you promised me my freedom. Please remember I have done you good service, told you no lies, made no mistakes, served you without grudge or grumbling.'

'How now!' said Prospero. 'You do not remember what a torment I freed you from. Have you forgotten the wicked witch Sycorax, who was almost bent double with age and envy? Where was she born? Speak! Tell me.'

'Sir, in Algiers,' said Ariel.

'O, was she?' said Prospero. 'I must remind you of what you have been when I find that you do not remember. This wicked witch Sycorax was banished from Algiers because of her witchcraft, too terrible for humans to hear about. She was left here by the sailors and, because you were too delicate a spirit to carry out her wicked commands, she shut you up in a tree, where I found you howling. Rembember, I freed you from this torment.'

'Pardon me, dear master,' said Ariel, ashamed to seem ungrateful; 'I will obey your orders.'

'Do so,' said Prospero, 'and I will set you free.' He then gave Ariel some more orders. Ariel went first to the place where he had left Ferdinand and found him still sitting on the grass in the same miserable position.

'O my young gentleman,' said Ariel, when he saw him, 'I will soon move you. You must be brought somewhere, I am told, for the Lady Miranda to catch sight of your fine looks. Come, sir, follow me.' He then began singing:

> *Full fathom five thy father lies;*
> *Of his bones are coral made;*
> *Those are pearls that were his eyes*
> *Nothing of him that doth fade*
> *But doth suffer a sea-change,*
> *Into something rich and strange.*
> *Sea-nymphs hourly ring his knell:*
> *Hark! now I hear them — Ding-dong, bell.*

This strange news of his lost father soon roused the prince from his dazed state. In amazement he followed the sound of Ariel's voice, till it led him to Prospero and Miranda, who were sitting under the shade of a large tree. Now, Miranda had never seen a man before, apart from her own father.

'Miranda,' said Prospero, 'tell me what you are looking at over there.'

'O father,' said Miranda, in surprise, 'surely that is a spirit. Lord! how it looks around! Believe me, sir, it is a beautiful creature. Is it not a spirit?'

'No, girl,' answered her father; 'it eats and sleeps, and has senses just like us. This young man you see was in the ship. His sadness has changed his looks, or you might call him a handsome person. He has lost his companions and is wandering about to find them.'

Miranda, who thought all men had grave faces and grey beards like her father, was delighted with the appearance of this handsome young prince; and Ferdinand seeing such a lovely woman in this deserted place and, from the strange sounds he had heard, expecting nothing but wonders, thought he was on an enchanted island, and that Miranda was the goddess of the place. So he began to speak to her as if she really were a goddess.

She answered timidly that she was not a goddess, but an ordinary girl, and was going to tell him all about herself, when Prospero interrupted her. He was pleased to find they liked each other, for he could plainly see that they had fallen in love at first sight. However, to test Ferdinand's faithfulness, he decided to throw some difficulties in their way. Stepping forward, he spoke to the prince, saying that he had come to the island as a spy to take it from its true lord, Prospero. 'Follow me,' he said. 'I will tie your neck and feet together. You shall drink seawater and your food shall be shellfish, withered roots and husks of acorns.

'No,' said Ferdinand, 'I will resist such entertainment till I see a more powerful enemy,' and drew his sword. Prospero, waving his magic wand, fixed him to the spot where he stood, so that he could not move a step.

Miranda held her father's arm saying, 'Why are you so unkind? Have pity, sir; I will be his surety. This is the second man I ever saw and to me he seems to be a true one.'

'Silence!' said her father. 'One word more will make me cross with you, girl. What sort of defence can you be for an impostor! You think there are no more such fine men when you have seen only him and Caliban. I tell you, foolish girl, most men outstrip him just as much as he outstrips Caliban.' He said this to test his daughter's faithfulness. She replied, 'Then I have simple tastes. I don't want to see a better man.'

'Come on, young man,' said Prospero to the prince, 'you have no power to disobey me.'

'I have not, indeed,' answered Ferdinand. He didn't realize that magic was what prevented him from resisting and was astonished to find himself so strangely forced to follow Prospero. Looking back at Miranda for as long as he could see her, he said, as he went after Prospero into the cave, 'My spirits are all muddled up, as if I were in a dream, but this man's threats and the weakness I feel would not matter at all if I might look out from my prison once a day to see this beautiful girl.'

Prospero didn't keep Ferdinand shut up inside the cell for very long. He soon brought his prisoner outside and set him to work, taking care to let his daughter know the hard job he had imposed on him. He then pretended to go into his study and secretly watched them both.

Prospero had ordered Ferdinand to pile up some heavy logs of wood. Kings' sons are not used to heavy work and Miranda soon found that her admirer was almost dying with exhaustion.

'O dear!' said she, 'do not work so hard. My father is at his studies; he will be busy for the next three hours. Please take a rest.'

'O my dear lady,' said Ferdinand, 'I dare not. I must finish my job before a have a rest.'

'If you sit down,' said Miranda, 'I will carry your logs for a while.' Ferdinand would not agree to this. Instead of a help, Miranda became a nuisance, for they began a long conversation so that the business of log-carrying went on very slowly.

Prospero, who had imposed this task merely as test of Ferdinand's love, was not at his books as his daughter supposed, but was standing by them, invisible, to overhear what they said.

Ferdinand asked her her name, which she told him, saying it was against her father's express command to tell him.

Prospero only smiled at this first instance of his daughter's disobedience because, having by his magic caused his daughter to fall in love suddenly, he was not angry that she showed her love by forgetting to obey him. Then he listened with pleasure while

Ferdinand told Miranda that he loved her more than all the ladies he had ever seen.

He told her that she was more beautiful than all the women in the world. She replied, 'I do not remember the face of any woman, nor have I seen any more men than you, my good friend, and my dear father. I don't know how other people look, but, believe me, sir, I do not want any companion in the world besides you, nor can I imagine anyone I could consider better-looking than you. But, sir, I am afraid that I talk to you too freely and I forget my father's instructions.'

At this, Prospero smiled and nodded his head, as much as to say, 'This proceeds exactly as I want it to; my girl will be Queen of Naples.'

Then Ferdinand, in another fine long speech (for young princes speak in courtly phrases), told Miranda that he was the heir to the crown of Naples and that she should be his queen.

'Oh, sir!' she said, 'I am silly to cry over something I am glad of. I will answer you clearly and truly. I will be your wife if you will marry me.'

Prospero prevented Ferdinand's thanks by making himself visible.

'Don't be afraid, my child,' he said; 'I have overheard and approve of all you have said. And, Ferdinand, if I have treated you too severely, I will make it up to you by giving you my daughter. All your troubles were only my test of your love and you have succeeded completely. Then as my gift, which your true love has fairly won, take my daughter, and do not smile that I boast she is beyond praise.' He then told them that he had business elsewhere and also suggested that they should sit down and talk together

till he returned. This was one order Miranda did not seem at all inclined to disobey.

After he had left them, Prospero called his spirit Ariel, who came quickly, eager to tell him what he had done with Prospero's brother and the King of Naples. Ariel said he had left them almost out of their minds with fear at the strange things he had made them see and hear. When they were tired out with wandering about and starving hungry, he suddenly set a delicious banquet in front of them. Just as they were going to eat, he had suddenly appeared at the table in the shape of a harpy, a voracious monster with wings and claws, and the feast had vanished. Then, to their utter amazement, the harpy had spoken to them, reminding them of their cruelty in driving Prospero from his dukedom and leaving him and his baby daughter to die in the sea. He had told them that these terrors were a punishment.

The King of Naples and Antonio, the cheating brother, were sorry for the injustice they had done to Prospero. Ariel told his master that he was certain their regret was sincere, and that he, although only a spirit, could not help pitying them.

'Then bring them here, Ariel,' said Prospero; 'if you, who are only a spirit, feel sorry for them, shall not I, who am also a human being like they are, feel sorry for them too? Bring them quickly, my dainty Ariel.'

Ariel soon returned with the king and Antonio. Old Gonzalo had also followed, wondering at the wild music Ariel played to draw them on to his master. Gonzalo was the man who had so kindly provided Prospero with books, food and water, when his wicked brother left him, as he thought, to die in an open boat on the sea.

Misery and terror had confused them so much that they did not recognize Prospero. The first person he told that he was really Prospero was the good old Gonzalo, calling him a life-saver. Then he told his brother and the king.

Antonio, with tears in his eyes and sad words of true regret, begged his brother's forgiveness. The king also said how truly sorry he was for having helped Antonio to steal his brother's throne. Prospero forgave them and, when they promised to give him back his dukedom, he said to the King of Naples, 'I have a gift in store for you too.' He opened the door and showed him his son Ferdinand playing chess with Miranda.

Nothing could be greater than the joy of the father and the son at this unexpected meeting, for they each thought the other had drowned in the storm.

'O wonder!' said Miranda. 'What fine people these are! It must surely be a magnificent world that has such people in it.'

The King of Naples was almost as astonished at the beauty and grace of Miranda as his son had been.

'Who is this girl?' he asked. 'She is like a goddess that separated us and then brought us together.'

'No, sir,' answered Ferdinand, smiling to find his father had made the same mistake that he had done when he first saw Miranda. 'She is a human, but by some special magic, she is mine. I chose her when I could not ask you, father, for your permission because I did not know you were still alive. She is the daughter of Prospero, who is the famous Duke of Milan. I have heard so much about him but never saw him till now. He has given me a new life and has made himself a second father to me giving me this dear girl.'

'Then I must be her father,' said the king; 'but, oh! how oddly it will sound for me to ask my children to forgive me.'

'No more of that,' said Prospero; 'let us forget our past troubles, as they have ended so happily.' Then Prospero hugged his brother and again assured him of his forgiveness. He said that a wise, overseeing Providence had permitted him to be driven from his poor dukedom of Milan so that his daughter might become Queen of Naples, for meeting on this desert island had made the king's son love Miranda.

These kind words, which Prospero meant to comfort his brother, filled Antonio with such shame and remorse that he cried and couldn't speak. Kind old Gonzalo cried as well to see this joyful reconciliation and prayed for blessing on the young couple.

Prospero now told them that their ship was safe in the harbour and the sailors all on board. He said that he and his daughter would accompany them home the next morning. 'In the meantime,' said he, 'have something to eat and drink — the best I can offer in this poor cave. To entertain you this evening I will tell you the story of my life from my first landing on this desert island.' He then called for Caliban to prepare some food and set the cave in order. Everyone was astonished at the uncouth form and savage appearance of this ugly monster, who (Prospero said) was his only servant.

Before Prospero left the island, he released Ariel from his service, to the great joy of that lively little spirit. Although he had been a faithful servant to his master, he was always longing to enjoy his freedom — to wander uncontrolled in the air like a wild bird, under green trees, among pleasant fruits and sweet-smelling flowers.

'My quaint Ariel,' said Prospero to the little sprite when he made him free, 'I shall miss you, but you shall have your freedom.'

'Thank you, my dear master,' said Ariel, 'but let me guide your ship home with fair winds, before you say goodbye to the assistance of your faithful spirit. Then, master, when I am free, how merrily I shall live!'

Here Ariel sang this pretty song:

> *Where the bee sucks, there suck I:*
> *In a cowslip's bell I lie;*
> *There I couch when owls do cry.*
> *On the bat's back I do fly*
> *After summer merrily.*
> *Merrily, merrily, shall I live now*
> *Under the blossom that hangs on the bough.*

Prospero then buried his wand deep in the earth and threw his magical books into the sea, for he had decided to give up his magic. Having overcome his enemies and having made friends again with his brother and the King of Naples, nothing was left to complete his happiness but to return to his own country. There he would take possession of his dukedom and go to the wedding of his daughter and Prince Ferdinand, which the king said should be celebrated with great splendour as soon as they reached Naples. Under the care of the spirit Ariel, they had a pleasant voyage, and soon arrived.

A Midsummer Night's Dream

There was a law in the ancient city of Athens which allowed fathers to force their daughters to marry men chosen by their parents. If a daughter refused to marry the man her father had chosen to be her husband, the father was allowed to have her put to death. Of course, fathers do not often want their own daughters to die, even if they are sometimes a little disobedient, so this law was seldom or never used. It is probable, however, that the young ladies of the city were often threatened by their parents with the terrors of it.

There was one time, however, when an old man called Egeus actually did come before Theseus, Duke of Athens, to complain of his daughter Hermia. He had ordered her to marry Demetrius, a young man of a noble Athenian family, but she refused to obey him because she loved another young Athenian who was called Lysander. Egeus demanded justice of Theseus and asked for this cruel law to be used against his daughter.

Hermia pleaded in excuse for her disobedience that Demetrius had previously said that he was in love with her best friend Helena and that Helena loved Demetrius to distraction. Although Hermia gave this good reason for not obeying her father, Egeus remained stern and unmoved.

Theseus, though a great and merciful prince, could not alter the laws of his country. He could only give Hermia four days to consider and at the end of that time, if she still refused to marry Demetrius, she was to be put to death.

When Hermia was dismissed from the duke's presence, she went to see Lysander and told him of her danger — she must either give him up and marry Demetrius or lose her life in four days' time.

Lysander was very upset when he heard this terrible news. Remembering that he had an aunt who lived at some distance from Athens and that where she lived the cruel law could not be used against Hermia (this law did not apply outside the city), he suggested to Hermia that she should creep out of her father's house that night and run away with him to his aunt's house, where he would marry her. 'I will meet you,' Lysander said, 'in the wood a few miles outside the city — the lovely wood where we once met Helena on the May morning.'

Hermia joyfully agreed to the plan. She told no one about it except her friend Helena. Girls will do silly things for love and Helena, unkindly, decided to go and tell Demetrius. She didn't have any hope that betraying her friend's secret would do her any good apart from the poor pleasure of following her faithless lover to the wood, for she knew quite well that Demetrius would chase after Hermia.

The wood where Lysander and Hermia planned to meet was the favourite place of those creatures known as Fairies. Oberon the king and Titania the queen of the fairies, with all their followers, held their midnight dances and parties in this wood.

The king and queen were at loggerheads at this time. They never met by moonlight in the shady walks of this pleasant wood but they started quarrelling, till all the countryside itself was in an uproar. The reason for this unhappy disagreement was that Titania refused to give Oberon a little changeling boy, whose mother had been Titania's friend. Upon her death, the fairy queen stole the child from its nurse and brought him up in the woods.

The night on which Hermia and Lysander planned to meet in this very wood, as Titania was walking with some of her maids od honour, she met Oberon attended by his train of fairy courtiers.

'How unfortunate to meet you in the moonlight, proud Titania,' said the fairy king.

The queen replied, 'What! is that you, jealous Oberon? Fairies, skip away from here. I have promised myself to have nothing to do with him.' 'Stay, rash fairy!' said Oberon, 'am I not your lord? Why does Titania cross her Oberon? Give me your little changeling boy to be my page.'

'Set your heart at rest,' answered the queen, 'your whole fairy kingdom would not buy the boy from me.' She then left Oberon in great anger. 'Well, go your way,' said Oberon, 'before the morning dawns I will punish you for this.'

Oberon then sent for Puck, his chief favourite and helper.

Puck, or, as he was sometimes called, Robin Goodfellow, was a clever and mischievous sprite that used to play tricks in the neighbouring villages — sometimes getting into the dairies and skimming the cream from the milk, sometimes hiding in the butter-churn so that the dairymaid would work without any success to change her cream into butter. The young men of the village didn't do any better, whenever Puck chose to play his tricks in the brewing vat, the ale was sure to be spoiled. When a few neighbours met for a sociable drink, Puck would jump into a tankard of ale in the likeness of a roasted crab apple and, just as some old woman was taking a sip, he would bob against her lips and spill the ale over her withered chin. When an old woman was about to sit down and tell her neighbours a sad story, Puck would disguise himself as a three-legged stool and slip out from under her. Down she toppled and all the old gossips would hold their sides and laugh at her, saying they never spent a merrier hour.

'Come here, Puck,' said Oberon to this merry wanderer of the night. 'Fetch me the flower which girls call "love in idleness". If you put the juice of that little purple flower on the eyelids of someone who is asleep, it will make him fall in love with the first person he sees when he wakes up. I will drop some of that juice on the eyelids of my Titania when she is asleep and when she opens her eyes, she will fall in love with whatever she sees even though it might be a lion or a bear, a meddling monkey or a busy ape. Before I take the charm from her sight, which I can do with another spell I know, I will make her give me the boy to be my page.'

Puck, who loved mischief, was really pleased with this plan and ran to look for the flower. While Oberon was waiting for him to return, he noticed Demetrius and Helena enter the wood. He overheard Demetrius telling her off for following him and saying very unkind things. Helena reminded him how he used to love her and tell her how true he was to her. He then left her, as he said, to the mercy of the wild beasts and she ran after him as fast as she could.

The fairy king, who was always friendly to true lovers, felt very sorry for Helena.

When Puck returned with the little purple flower, Oberon said to him, 'Take a part of this flower. A sweet Athenian lady, who is in love with a young man who doesn't care about her, has been here. If you find him sleeping, drop some of the love-juice in his eyes, but try to do it when she is near him so that she will be the first thing he sees when he wakes.' Puck promised to manage this matter very skilfully.

Then without her noticing, Oberon went to Titania's bower, where she was preparing to sleep. Her fairy bower was a bank, covered with wild thyme, cowslips and sweet violets under a canopy of woodbine, musk-roses and eglantine. Titania always rested for a part of the night there. Her coverlet was the patterned skin of a snake, which, though small, was wide enough to wrap a fairy in.

He found Titania giving orders to her fairies of what they were to do while she slept. 'Some of you,' said Her Majesty, 'must kill cankers in the musk-rose buds and some wage war with the bats for their leather wings to make my small elves coats, and some of you keep watch so that the noisy owl that nightly hoots does not come near me. First, sing me to sleep.' Then they began to sing this song:

You spotted snakes with double tongue
Thorny hedgehogs, be not seen;
Newts and blind-worms, do no wrong,
Come not near our fairy queen.
Philomel, with melody,
Sing in our sweet lullaby,
Lulla, lulla, lullaby; lulla, lulla, lullaby:
Never harm,
Nor spell, nor charm,
Come our lovely lady nigh;
So good night with lullaby.

When the fairies had sung their queen to sleep with this pretty lullaby, they left her to get on with the important jobs she had given them. Oberon quietly approached Titania and dropped some of the love-juice on her eyelids, saying:

What thou seest when thou dost wake,
Do it for thy true-love take.

Meanwhile, Hermia had made her escape from her father's house that night to avoid the death she was doomed to for refusing to marry Demetrius. When she entered the wood, she found her beloved Lysander waiting for her, to take her to his aunt's house. Before they had travelled halfway through the wood, Hermia was so tired that Lysander, who took great care of her, persuaded her to rest till the morning on a bank of soft moss. He lay down on the ground a little way off and they both soon fell fast asleep. Here they were found by Puck. He, seeing a handsome young man asleep and noting that his clothes were made in the Athenian fashion, and seeing a pretty young lady sleeping near him, assumed that this must be the couple whom Oberon had sent him to find. Naturally enough he reckoned that, as they were alone together, she must be the first he would see when he awoke. So without further delay, he poured some of the juice of the little purple flower on Lysander's eyelids. Unfortunately, just at the moment Lysander woke up, Helena, who had got lost while chasing Demetrius, came along. So Helena, not Hermia, was the first person Lysander saw when he opened his eyes. The love-charm was so powerful that all his love for Hermia vanished and Lysander instantly fell in love with Helena.

If he had seen Hermia first when he awoke, Puck's blunder would not have mattered for he could not love that faithful lady too well. For poor Lysander to be forced by a fairy love-charm to forget his own true Hermia and to run after another lady, leaving Hermia asleep quite alone in a wood at midnight, was a sad chance indeed.

This is what had happened. Helena tried to keep up with Demetrius when he so rudely ran away, but she could not. She soon lost sight of him and, as she was wandering about, miserable and lonely, she arrived at the place where Lysander was sleeping. 'Ah!' she said, 'this is Lysander lying on the ground. Is he dead or asleep?' Then, gently touching him, she said, 'Good sir, if you are alive, wake up.' Upon this Lysander opened his eyes and because the love-charm began to work, immediately spoke to her in terms of extravagant love and admiration. He told her that she was much more beautiful than Hermia as a dove is more beautiful than a raven. He said that he would run through fire for her and made many more such lover-like speeches. Helena, knowing Lysander was her friend and Hermia's lover and that he was solemnly engaged to marry her, was furious when she heard him. She thought (as well she might) that Lysander was making fun of her. 'Oh!' she said, 'why was I born to be mocked and scorned by everyone? Is it not enough, is it not enough, young man, that I can never get a gentle look or a kind word from Demetrius, but you, sir, must pretend in this mocking way to love me? I thought, Lysander, you were kinder than that.' Enraged, she ran away and Lysander followed her, quite forgetting his own Hermia, who was still asleep.

When Hermia awoke all alone, she was frightened. She wandered about the wood, not knowing what had happened to Lysander or which way to go to find him. In the meantime, Demetrius, not being able to find Hermia and his rival Lysander and tired with his fruitless search, had fallen asleep. Oberon had learned from questioning Puck that he had applied the love-charm to the wrong person's eyes. Now, finding Demetrius, Oberon touched his eyelids with the love-juice. He woke up instantly and the first person he saw was — Helena. Just as Lysander had done before, Demetrius began telling her how much he loved her. At that moment, Lysander, followed by Hermia (for through Puck's unlucky mistake it was now Hermia's turn to run after her lover), came running up. Then Lysander and Demetrius, both speaking at the same time, told Helena how much they loved her. Both of them were under the influence of the same potent charm.

Poor Helena was astonished and thought that Demetrius, Lysander and her once best friend Hermia were all in plot together to make fun of her.

Hermia was as much surprised as Helena. She didn't know why Lysander and Demetrius, who both loved her before, were now in love with Helena. To Hermia the matter did not seem to be fun at all.

Hermia and Helena, who before had always been best friends, now started saying horrid things to each other.

'Unkind Hermia,' said Helena, 'you were the one who set Lysander on to upset me with mock praises; and your other lover Demetrius, who used almost to kick me with his foot — you made him call me "goddess", "nymph", "rare", "precious" and "celestial". He would not say these things to me, because he hates me, if you did not set him on to make fun of me. Unkind Hermia to join with men in scorning your poor friend. Have you forgotten the friendship of our schooldays? How often, Hermia, did the two of us used to sit on one cushion, both singing one song, with our needles embroidering the same flower on the same sampler, growing up together like twins? Hermia, it is neither friendly, nor ladylike to join with men in scorning your poor friend.'

'I am amazed at your angry words,' said Hermia. 'I am not mocking you; it seems that you are mocking me.'

'Oh, yes!' returned Helena. 'Keep it up, pretend to look serious and then make faces at me when I turn my back; then wink at each other and keep the joke going. If you had any pity, grace or manners, you would not treat me like this.'

While Helena and Hermia were speaking these angry words to each other, Demetrius and Lysander left them to fight each other over Helena.

When Helena and Hermia found the men had left them, they set off again and once more wandered wearily in the wood in search of their lovers.

As soon as they were gone, the fairy king, who, together with Puck, had been listening to their quarrels, said 'Was all this a mistake, Puck, or did you play a trick?'

'Believe me, king of shadows,' answered Puck, 'it was a mistake. Didn't you tell me I should know the man by his Athenian clothes? However, I am not sorry it has happened, for I think their carryings-on are very funny.'

'You heard,' Oberon said, 'that Demetrius and Lysander have gone to find a convenient place to fight. I order you to blanket the night with a thick fog and lead these quarrelsome lovers so far apart in the dark that they won't be able to find each other. Mimic their voices to each other and make it sound like they're daring each other, so that they follow you. Do this till they are so tired they can't go on. When they fall asleep, drop the juice of this other flower into Lysander's eyes. When he awakes, he will have forgotten his new love for Helena and return to his old love for Hermia. Then the two pretty girls will each be happy with the man she loves and they will think all that has happened was a bad dream. Get on with this quickly, Puck, and I will go and see what sweet love my Titania has found.'

Titania was still sleeping. Near her, there was a workman, a weaver, who had lost his way in the wood and was also asleep. 'This fellow,' Oberon said, 'shall be my Titania's true love.' He magically fixed an ass's head over the weaver's; it seemed to fit him so well it might have grown upon his own shoulders. Although Oberon fixed on the ass's head very gently, it woke the weaver up, and unconscious of what Oberon had done to him, he wandered towards the bower where the fairy queen slept.

'Oh! what angel is that I see?' said Titania, opening her eyes. The juice of the little purple flower was beginning to take effect. 'Are you as wise as you are handsome?'

'Why, madam,' said the foolish weaver, 'if I have enough brains to find the way out of this wood, I have as many as I want.'

'Don't wish yourself out of the wood,' said the love-struck queen. 'I am not an ordinary spirit. I love you. Come with me and I will give you fairies to look after you.' She then called four of her fairies. Their names were Peaseblossom, Cobweb, Moth and Mustardseed.

The queen said, 'Look after this sweet gentleman. Hop in his walks and skip in his sight. Feed him with grapes and apricots and steal the honey-bags from the bees for him. 'Come, sit with me,' she said to the weaver, 'and let me stroke your lovely hairy cheeks, my darling, and kiss your beautiful long ears.'

'Where is Peaseblossom?' said the ass-headed man, not much impressed by the fairy queen's courtship but very proud of his new attendants.

'Here, sir,' said Peaseblossom.

'Scratch my head,' said the weaver, whose name was Bottom. 'Where is Cobweb?'

'Here, sir,' said Cobweb.

'Good Mr Cobweb,' said the foolish man, 'bring me the honey-bag from the red humble-bee on the top of that thistle over there. Do not go for too much trouble, Mr Cobweb, and take care that the honey-bag does not break. I should be sorry if you were drowned in honey. Where is Mustardseed?'

'Here, sir,' said Mustardseed. 'What can I do for you?'

'Nothing, good Mr Mustardseed,' said Bottom, 'but help Mr Peaseblossom to scratch. I must go to a barber's for a shave, Mr Mustardseed, for I think I am astonishingly hairy about the face.'

'My sweet love,' said the queen, 'what would you like to eat? I have a brave fairy who shall find the squirrel's hoard and fetch you some new nuts.'

'I would rather have a handful of dried peas,' said Bottom who had got an ass's appetite with his ass's head, 'but, please, let none of your people disturb me, for I think I'd like a sleep.'

'Sleep, then,' said the queen, 'and I will wrap my arms around you. O how I love you! How I adore you!'

When the fairy king saw the weaver sleeping in the arms of his queen, he came up to her and scolded her with having lavished her love upon an ass. She could not deny it, as the weaver was lying there asleep in her arms with his ass's head crowned by her with flowers. When Oberon had teased her for some time, he again asked her to give him the changeling boy and she did so.

Oberon, having obtained the little boy to be his page, took pity on the disgraceful situation. He poured some of the juice of the other flower on to Titania's eyelids and the fairy queen immediately recovered her senses. She was amazed at the sight of Bottom and said how she now loathed the sight of the strange monster.

Oberon ordered Puck to take the ass's head from Bottom and leave him to finish his nap with his own fool's head upon his shoulders.

Oberon and Titania were now good friends again. He told her the story of the young lovers and their midnight quarrels and she agreed to go with him to see the end of their adventures.

The fairy king and queen found the four Athenians asleep on the grass quite near each other. Puck, to make up for his mistake, had worked hard to bring them all to the same place without anyone realizing the others were there. He had carefully removed the charm from Lysander's eyes with the juice the fairy king had given to him.

Hermia awoke first and, finding her lost Lysander asleep so near her, was looking at him and wondering at his strange unfaithfulness. Lysander opening his eyes and seeing his dear Hermia, came to his senses, his love for Hermia flooded back. They began to talk over the adventures of the night, wondering if these things had really happened or if they had both been dreaming the same bewildering dream.

Helena and Demetrius were awake by this time. Sleep had calmed Helena's anger and she listened with delight when Demetrius told her again how much he loved her. To her surprise as well as her pleasure, she began to realize that he meant what he was saying.

The two girls, now no longer rivals, once more became best friends. All the unkind words they had said to each other were forgiven and they calmly discussed what was the best thing to do in their present situation. It was soon agreed that, as Demetrius had given up his claim to Hermia, he should try to persuade her father to take back the cruel sentence of death passed against her. Demetrius was preparing to return to Athens to do this, when they were all surprised by the sight of Egeus, Hermia's father, who came to the wood following his runaway daughter.

When Egeus understood that Demetrius no longer wanted to marry his daughter, he no longer opposed her marriage to Lysander. He agreed that they should be married in four days' time, that being the day when Hermia had been condemned to lose her life. Helena joyfully agreed to marry her beloved and now faithful Demetrius on the same day.

The fairy king and queen, who were invisible spectators of this happy ending, were so much pleased that they decided to celebrate the wedding with sports and games throughout their fairy kingdom.

And now, if you are offended by this story of fairies and their pranks, just imagine that you have been asleep and dreaming. All these adventures were just visions you saw in your sleep. It was all a Midsummer Night's Dream.

Much Ado About Nothing

T he palace at Messina was the home of the governor, Leonato, his daughter, Hero, and his niece, Beatrice. Beatrice was a lively girl and loved to amuse her more serious cousin Hero with her witty conversation. Whatever was going on provided lighthearted Beatrice with something amusing to say.

At the time the story of these two ladies begins, some young soldiers were passing through Messina on their way from a war. They had all shown great bravery and had now come to visit Leonato. Among them were Don Pedro, the Prince of Arragon, and his friend Claudio, who was a lord of Florence. Also with them was the wild and witty Benedick, and he was a lord of Padua.

They had all been to Messina before and the hospitable governor reintroduced them to his daughter and his niece as old friends.

The moment Benedick entered the room, he began a lively conversation with Leonato and the prince. Beatrice, who did not like to be left out of any talk, interrupted Benedick by saying, 'I wonder why you are still talking, Signior Benedick; nobody is listening to you.' Benedick was just as much a chatterbox as Beatrice, but he was not very pleased at this greeting. He thought it was not suitable for a well-brought-up lady to be so flippant and he remembered that when he was last at Messina Beatrice used to pick him to be the butt of her jokes. Nobody dislikes being made fun of more than someone who likes to make fun of other people. So it was with Benedick and Beatrice. These two sharp wits never met without making jokes at each other's expense and they always parted feeling cross with each other. So, when Beatrice stopped him in the middle of his conversation by telling him that nobody was listening to what he was saying, Benedick pretended that he had not noticed that she was there. He said, 'What, my dear Miss Mockery, are you still alive?'

Now a battle broke out between them all over again and a fast, fierce argument followed. Although Beatrice knew he had proved himself as being very brave in the war that had just ended, she said she would eat all he had killed there, suggesting he was a coward. Observing the prince's delight in Benedick's witty conversation, she called him 'the prince's jester'. This sarcasm sank deeper into Benedick's mind than everything else Beatrice had said. Hinting that he was a coward did not worry him at all as he knew himself to be a brave man, but there is nothing that great wits dread so much as the accusation of silliness, because the charge comes sometimes a little too near the truth. Benedick really resented Beatrice when she called him 'the prince's jester'.

Hero, who was a modest young woman, was silent before the noble guests. Claudio watched Hero and noticed how beautiful and elegant she had grown since he had last seen her. Meanwhile, the prince was highly amused by the humorous conversation between Beatrice and Benedick and he whispered to Leonato, 'This is a lively young woman. She would make an excellent wife for Benedick.'

Leonato replied, 'O my lord, my lord, if they were married they would talk themselves mad within a week.' Though Leonato thought they would make an unsuitable couple, the prince did not give up the idea of matching these two sharp wits together.

When the prince and Claudio returned from the palace, it became clear that a marriage between Benedick and Beatrice was not the only one that was in people's minds, for Claudio talked so glowingly of Hero that the prince guessed what was happening in his heart. He was delighted and said to Claudio, 'Do you love Hero?'

Claudio replied, 'When I was in Messina before I looked at her with a soldier's eye. In other words, I liked her but had no time for loving because of the war. Now in this happy time of peace, thoughts of war do not have to occupy my mind and gentle delicate thoughts have taken their place. I keep thinking how beautiful young Hero is and remembering that I liked her before I went to the wars.' Claudio's admission that he loved Hero seemed so important to the prince that he lost no time in asking Leonato to accept Claudio as a son-in-law. Leonato agreed. The prince found no difficulty in persuading gentle Hero to listen to Claudio's proposal for he was a talented and charming man. Claudio, assisted by his kind prince, soon persuaded Leonato to set an early date for the wedding.

Claudio had to wait only a few days before he was to be married to his lovely bride, but he complained that the waiting was tedious; indeed, most young men are impatient when they are waiting for something they have set their hearts on. To make the time seem shorter the prince suggested that they should devise a trick to make Benedick and Beatrice fall in love with each other to keep them amused. Claudio thought this was a splendid idea, and Leonato promised them his help. Even Hero said she would do any small thing to help her cousin find a good husband.

The trick the prince invented was that the men should make Benedick believe that Beatrice was in love with him, and that Hero should make Beatrice believe that Benedick was in love with her.

The prince, Leonato and Claudio began their plan first. They found their chance when Benedick was sitting quietly reading in the garden. The prince and his assistants

took up their places among the trees behind Benedick so that he would overhear all they said. After chatting for a moment or two, the prince said, 'Come here, Leonato. What was it you told me the other day — that your niece Beatrice is in love with Signior Benedick? I never believed that lady would love any man.'

'No, nor did I, my lord,' answered Leonato. 'It is quite amazing that she should so adore Benedick because she always behaves as if she disliked him.'

Claudio also said that all this was true and that Hero had told him Beatrice was so in love with Benedick and that she would die of misery if he could not be persuaded to love her. Leonato and Claudio seemed to agree this was impossible because Benedick had always criticized all pretty girls and Beatrice in particular.

The prince pretended to hear all this with great pity for Beatrice and he said, 'It would be a good thing if Benedick were told about this.'

'What for?' asked Claudio. 'He would only make a joke of it and torment the poor lady worse.'

'If he does,' said the prince, 'it would be a good deed to hang him, for Beatrice is a very sweet girl and very sensible in every way except in loving Benedick.' Then the prince waved to his companions to walk on and leave Benedick to think about what he had overheard.

Benedick had been listening to this conversation with great eagerness. When he heard that Beatrice loved him, he said to himself, 'Is it possible? Is that really how the wind blows?' When they were gone he began to reason with himself: 'This can't be a trick! They were very serious. They have the truth from Hero and seemed to pity the lady. Love me! Then, I must love her back! I never thought I would marry. But when I said I should die a bachelor, I thought I would be killed in the war and not live to be married. They say the lady is good and beautiful. And wise in everything except in loving me. Why, that is not a good argument to prove she is silly. But here comes Beatrice. She certainly is pretty. She does look as though she is in love.' Beatrice now came towards him and said with her usual sharpness, 'Against my will I am sent to ask you to come in to dinner.' Benedick, who had never before felt inclined to speak so politely to her, replied, 'Beatrice, thank you for bothering.' When Beatrice, after two or three more rude comments left him, Benedick thought he had noticed a hidden kindness in her impolite words. He said aloud, 'If I do not take pity on her, I am a villain. I will go and get her picture.'

Benedick being caught in the net they had spread for him, it was now Hero's turn to play her part with Beatrice. She sent for Ursula and Margaret, two women who looked after her. She said to Margaret, 'Margaret, run to the parlour where you will find my cousin Beatrice chatting with the prince and Claudio. Whisper in her ear that Ursula and I are walking in the orchard and talking about her. Tell her to hide in that pleasant shady place surrounded by honeysuckles.' This was the very same place as that where Benedick had just been such an attentive listener.

'I will make her come at once, I'm sure,' said Margaret.

Hero took Ursula with her into the orchard and said to her, 'Now, Ursula, when Beatrice comes, we will walk up and down this alley and talk about Benedick. When I say his name you must praise him more than any man deserves. I will then tell you how Benedick is in love with Beatrice. Now begin for Beatrice is racing like a lapwing across the ground to hear what we are saying.' They began. Hero started, answering something Ursula had already said, 'No, truly, Ursula. She is too scornful.'

'But are you sure,' said Ursula, 'that Benedick loves Beatrice so completely?'

Hero replied, 'That is what the prince and my lord Claudio said, and they begged me to tell her, but I persuaded them that if they were fond of Benedick, they should never let Beatrice know he loves her.'

'Certainly,' replied Ursula, 'it would not be a good thing for her to know about his love, because she would make a joke of it.'

'Why, to tell the truth,' said Hero, 'I have never seen a man, however wise, noble young or good looking, that she wouldn't criticize.'

'Very true, such nagging is not good,' said Ursula.

'No,' replied Hero; 'but who would dare tell her so? If I should speak, she would mock me into air.'

'Oh, you wrong your cousin,' Ursula said. 'She cannot be so lacking in judgement that she would refuse so fine a man as Signior Benedick.'

'He has a good reputation,' Hero said, 'indeed, he is the best man in Italy apart from my dear Claudio.' Hero gave her maid a hint that it was time to change the subject.

Ursula said, 'And when are you to be married, madam?' Hero then told her that the wedding would be the next day, and asked her to go in with her and look at some new clothes, as she wanted her advice on what to wear.

Beatrice, who had been listening breathlessly, exclaimed, 'My ears are burning! Can this be true? Goodbye contempt and scorn and goodbye girlish pride! Benedick, love on! I will love you back, taming my wild heart to your loving hand.'

It must have been a pleasant sight to see these old enemies changed into new and loving friends and to see their first meeting after being cheated into liking each other by the merry trick of the good-humoured prince. However, a sad reverse in the fortunes of Hero now took place. The next day, which was to have been her wedding day, brought sorrow to the heart of Hero and her good father Leonato.

The prince had a half-brother, who had also come from the wars to Messina. This brother, Don John, was a miserable, discontented man, who used his energy in doing wicked things. He hated the prince, his brother, and he hated Claudio because he was the prince's friend. He was determined to prevent Claudio's marriage to Hero, just for the spiteful pleasure of making Claudio and the prince unhappy. He knew that the prince had set his heart upon this marriage almost as much as Claudio himself. He employed a man called Borachio, who was as bad as he was himself, offering him a great reward. Borachio was in love with Margaret, Hero's attendant, and Don John, knowing this, persuaded him to make Margaret promise to talk with him from her lady's bedroom window that night after Hero was asleep. He was also to make her dress herself

in Hero's clothes. Don John wanted to deceive Claudio into the belief that it was Hero who was talking at the window.

Don John then went to the prince and Claudio and told them that Hero was disloyal and that she talked with men from her bedroom window at midnight. Now this was the evening before the wedding and he offered to take them that night to hear Hero chatting to a man from her window. They agreed to go along with him and Claudio said, 'If I see anything tonight which means I should not marry her, tomorrow in church I will shame her.'

The prince also said, 'And as I helped you to obtain her agreement to marry you, I will join with you to disgrace her.'

When Don John brought them near Hero's bedroom that night, they saw Borachio standing under the window and Margaret looking out of it. They heard her talking lovingly to Borachio and, as she was dressed in the same clothes they had seen Hero wear, the prince and Claudio believed it was Hero herself.

Nothing could equal Claudio's anger when he had made this discovery. All his love for the innocent Hero was at once changed into hatred and he decided to expose her unfaithfulness in church the next day as he had said he would. The prince agreed to this, thinking no punishment could be too severe for a woman who talked of love with another man the very night before she was going to be married to the noble Claudio.

The next day, they were all met to celebrate the wedding. Claudio and Hero were standing before the priest when Claudio, in the angriest language, accused poor blameless Hero. She was amazed at the strange words and meekly asked, 'Is my lord not feeling well that he speaks so strangely?'

Leonato, in the utmost horror, said to the prince, 'My lord, why don't you say something?'

'What should I say?' asked the prince. 'I feel I have let down my own good name by linking my dear friend to an unworthy woman. Leonato, in all honesty, my brother, poor Claudio and I saw and heard her last night at midnight talk with a man at her bedroom window.'

Benedick, astonished at what he heard, said, 'This doesn't look much like a wedding.'

'True,' replied the heartbroken Hero and then sank down in a dead faint. The prince and Claudio left the church without staying to see if Hero would recover or taking any notice of Leonato's distress. Their anger had made them totally hard-hearted.

Benedick remained and helped Beatrice bring Hero round from her faint, saying, 'How is she?'

'Dead, I think,' replied Beatrice in real misery, for she loved her cousin. She knew how good and honest Hero was so she believed nothing of the story the prince and Claudio had told. Leonato, on the other hand, believed the story of his child's shame and it was dreadful to hear him crying over her. She lay stiff as if she were dead and he wished that she might never open her eyes again.

The old priest was a wise man and knew a lot about human nature. He had watched Hero's face when she heard herself accused. First, she had blushed as if she were ashamed of herself and then he had seen an angel-like whiteness chase away those blushes. He had seen a fire in her eyes that denied the mistaken lie that the prince told. He said to the sorrowing father, 'You can call me a fool and not trust my reading, my observation, my age, my reverence, or my calling as a priest, if this sweet lady is not lying here innocent under some terrible error.'

When Hero recovered from the faint, the priest said to her, 'Lady, who is the man you are accused of talking words of love to at night?' Hero replied, 'The people who accused me know who he is. I know of no one.' Turning to Leonato, she said, 'O father, if you can prove that any man has ever talked to me at unsuitable times or that I exchanged words with any one at all last night, refuse me, hate me, torture me to death.'

'There is,' the priest said, 'some strange misunderstanding on the part of the prince and Claudio. He advised Leonato to say that Hero was dead. The dead faint in which they had left her would make this easy to believe. He also advised him to wear mourning clothes, erect a monument for her and prepare a funeral.

'What will that achieve?' said Leonato; 'what good will it do?'

The priest replied, 'The news of her death will change the lies into pity. That is some good, but not all the good I hope for. When Claudio hears that she died on hearing his words, he will remember her when she was alive. Then if he ever truly loved her, he will wish he had not accused her even though he thought his accusation true.'

Benedick now said, 'Leonato let the priest advise you. You know how fond I am of the prince and Claudio, yet I promise I will not reveal this secret to them.'

Leonato gave in. The kind priest led him and Hero away to comfort and console them. Beatrice and Benedick remained alone. This was the meeting which their friends, who devised the merry plot against them, expected to be such fun — those friends who were now overwhelmed with troubles and from whose minds all thoughts of merriment seemed forever banished.

Benedick spoke first. 'Beatrice, have you been crying all this time?'

'Yes, and I will cry a while longer,' said Beatrice.

'Truly,' said Benedick, 'I believe your cousin was wronged.'

'Ah!' said Beatrice, 'the man who would right her wrong would earn from me whatever he wanted!'

Benedick then said, 'Is there any way to show such friendship? I love no one in the world so much as I love you. Isn't that strange?'

'I could also say,' Beatrice said, 'that I love no one in the world so well as I love you; but don't believe me although I am not lying. I admit nothing and I deny nothing. I am sorry for my cousin.'

'By my sword,' said Benedick, 'you love me, and I tell you I love you. Come, ask me to do anything for you.'

'Kill Claudio,' Beatrice said.

'No! not for all the world,' said Benedick. He loved his friend Claudio and believed he had been imposed upon.

'Isn't Claudio a villain that has slandered, scorned and dishonoured my cousin?' said Beatrice. 'O, I wish I were a man!'

'Listen to me, Beatrice!' said Benedick, but Beatrice would hear nothing in Claudio's defence and she continued to urge Benedick to revenge her cousin's wrongs.

She said, 'Talk with a man out of the window — likely story! Sweet Hero! she is

wronged; she is slandered; she is ruined. O, I wish I were a man for Claudio's sake! or that I had any friend who act like a man for my sake! But courage is melted into sweet words and compliments. I cannot be a man with wishing, so I will die a woman with grieving.'

'Stay, Beatrice,' Benedick said. 'By this hand, I love you.'

'Use it for my love in some other way than swearing by it,' said Beatrice.

'Do you truly believe that Claudio has wronged Hero?' Benedick asked.

'Yes,' Beatrice answered, 'as sure as I have a thought or a soul.'

'Enough,' said Benedick, 'I will do as you ask. I will challenge him. I will kiss your hand and so leave you. By this hand Claudio shall pay me a dear account! As you hear from me, so think of me. Go, comfort your cousin.'

While Beatrice was pleading with Benedick rousing him to take Hero's side to fight his friend Claudio, Leonato was challenging the prince and Claudio. He wanted to make them pay for the injury they had done to his child, who, he told them, had died of misery. They had too much respect for his age and his sorrow to fight a duel and they said, 'No, do not quarrel with us, good old man.'

Then Benedick came and challenged Claudio to answer with his sword for the injury he had done to Hero. Claudio and the prince said to each other, 'Beatrice has set him on to do this.' Claudio would have accepted Benedick's challenge if the justice of Heaven had not at the moment brought better proof of Hero's innocence than the uncertain chances of a duel.

While the prince and Claudio were still discussing Benedick's challenge, a magistrate brought Borachio as a prisoner before the prince. Borachio had been overheard discussing the mischief Don John had employed him to do.

Borachio admitted to the prince, in Claudio's hearing, that it was Margaret dressed in Hero's clothes who had talked to him from the window. Claudio and the prince realized that Hero was innocent. If any doubt remained, it was removed by the flight of Don John. When he knew he had been found out, he ran away from Messina to avoid the just anger of his brother.

Claudio was heartbroken when he discovered that he had falsely accused Hero, whom he believed had died upon hearing his cruel word. The memory of his beloved Hero overcame him. The prince asked him if what he heard from Borachio felt like a sword through his body. He answered that he felt as if he had taken poison while Borachio was speaking.

Claudio begged Leonato for forgiveness for the injury he had done to his child. He promised to carry out whatever penance Leonato would lay upon him for his fault in believing the false accusation against his betrothed wife. For her dear sake, he would endure it.

The penance Leonato gave him was that he must marry Hero's cousin the next morning. He said that she was now his heir and looked very like Hero. Claudio, keeping the solemn promise he made to Leonato, said he would marry this unknown lady even if she were as ugly as a witch. His heart was very sad and he spent that night in tears at the tomb which Leonato had erected for Hero.

When morning came, the prince went to the church with Claudio, where the good priest, Leonato and his niece were already assembled to celebrate a second wedding. Leonato introduced Claudio to his promised bride. She was wearing a mask so that Claudio could not see her face. Claudio said to the lady in the mask, 'Give me your hand, before this holy priest. I will be your husband if you will marry me.'

'And, when I lived, I was your other wife,' said the unknown lady. Taking off her mask, she proved to be no niece, but Leonato's own daughter, Hero herself.

Claudio, who had thought her dead, could hardly believe his eyes. The prince, who was equally amazed, exclaimed, 'Is not this Hero, Hero who was dead?'

Leonato replied, 'She died, my lord, only as long as the lying stories about her lived.' The priest promised them an explanation of this miracle after the ceremony had ended. He was proceeding with the wedding service when he was interrupted by Benedick, who wanted to be married to Beatrice at the same time. Beatrice was not so sure. Benedick challenged her with her love for him, which he had learned about from Hero. Then all was explained; they discovered they had both been tricked into believing a love which had never existed. They had become true lovers by the power of a false joke, for their affection had grown too strong to be shaken off. Benedick kept up the joke and swore to Beatrice that he took her only out of pity and because he heard she was dying of love for him. Beatrice claimed that she agreed upon great persuasion and partly to save his life, for she had heard he was in a consumption. So this quarrelsome couple made a match of it after Claudio and Hero were married. To complete the story, Don John was caught and brought back to Messina. It was a suitable punishment for this gloomy, discontented man to see the joy and feasting which, in spite of his plotting, took place at the palace in Messina.

As You Like It

When France was divided into dukedoms, one of them was ruled by a usurper, who had stolen the dukedom from his elder brother. The lawful duke had been driven from his lands to the Forest of Arden. Here, the good duke lived with his close friends, who had put themselves into voluntary exile for his sake. This meant that their lands and money enriched the false duke. They soon grew used to the relaxed life they led here and found it pleasanter than the pomp and uneasy splendour of the court. Many young men from the court joined them and the time passed very pleasantly. In summer, they stretched out under the shade of the large forest trees, watching the wild deer play. They grew so fond of these silly dappled animals that they were sorry when they had to kill them for food. When the cold winds of winter made the duke feel this change of fortune, he put up with them patiently, saying, 'These cold winds blowing my body are true counsellors. They do not flatter, but truly present my condition to me. Although they bite sharply, their tooth is nothing like so keen as that biting hurt of unkindness and ingratitude. Good use can be made of unfortunate circumstances.' In this way the patient duke drew a useful moral from everything that he saw. In this life, remote from public places, he could find conversation in the sounds of trees, ideas in running water and good in everything.

The banished duke had a daughter called Rosalind. The usurping Duke Frederick still kept her at his court as a friend for his own daughter Celia. The two girls were very close friends and the disagreement between their fathers did not spoil their affection. Celia took every opportunity to make up to Rosalind for her father's injustice to Rosalind's. Whenever thoughts of her father's banishment and her own dependence on her uncle made Rosalind sad, Celia's whole care was to comfort and console her.

One day, when Celia was talking to Rosalind in her usual kind way, saying, 'Please, Rosalind, my sweet cousin, be merry,' a messenger from the duke entered. He had come to tell them that if they wished to see a wrestling match that was just going to begin, they must come at once to the courtyard in front of the palace. Celia, thinking it would amuse Rosalind, agreed to go and see it.

In those days wrestling was a favourite sport, so Celia and Rosalind went to watch. They found that it was likely to prove a very tragic sight, for a large, powerful champion who had already injured and killed many challengers, was just going to wrestle with a very young and inexperienced man, who would almost certainly be killed.

When the duke saw Celia and Rosalind, he said, 'Hallo, daughter and niece, have you come to see the wrestling? You will take little delight in it; the two men are so unequally matched. Out of pity for this young man, I would like to persuade him not to compete. Speak to him, girls, and see if you can persuade him.'

They were pleased to undertake this humane task. First Celia begged the young stranger to withdraw from the attempt. Then Rosalind spoke so kindly to him and with such feeling about the danger he was in that, instead of being persuaded to withdraw from the contest, all his thoughts were concentrated on showing his courage to this lovely young woman. He refused to back out in such charming and modest words, that the two girls felt even more worried about him. He ended his refusal by saying, 'I am sorry to deny such beautiful and excellent ladies anything. But let your pretty eyes and gentle wishes go with me to my trial of strength. If I lose, then I shall be shamed, but I was never gracious in the first place. If I am killed, it doesn't matter, because I am willing to die. I shan't upset my friends because I haven't got any. My death won't make the world a poorer place for I have nothing; I only fill up a place in the world which may be used by something better when I have made it empty.'

The wrestling match began. Celia hoped the young man would not be hurt, but Rosalind felt most for him. His friendless state and the way he said he wished to die made Rosalind think that he was like herself, unlucky. She pitied him so much and was so concerned about his danger while he was wrestling, that she might be almost said to have fallen in love with him at that moment.

The kindness of the two girls gave the unknown young man courage and strength so that he performed wonders. In the end he totally defeated the duke's wrestler, who was so winded that he was unable to speak or move for a while.

The Duke Frederick was delighted with the young stranger's courage and skill and asked his name and family, meaning to take him under his protection. The stranger said his name was Orlando and that he was the youngest son of Sir Rowland de Boys. Sir Rowland had been dead for some years, but when he was living, he had been a true subject and dear friend of the banished duke. When Frederick heard Orlando was the son of his banished brother's friend, all his liking for this brave young man was changed into displeasure. He left the place in a very bad temper. Hating to hear the very name of any of his brother's friends and yet still admiring Orlando's bravery, he said, as he went out, that he wished Orlando had been the son of any other man.

Rosalind was delighted to hear that her new favourite was the son of her father's old friend. She said to Celia, 'My father loved Sir Rowland de Boys and if I had known this young man was his son, I would have added tears to my pleading before he should have tried his strength.'

The girls then went up to him, and seeing him hurt by the duke's sudden displeasure, they spoke kind and encouraging words to him. When they were going away, Rosalind turned back to say some nice things to the brave young son of her father's friend. Taking a chain from round her neck, she said, 'Wear this for me. I am out of luck at the moment or I would give you a more valuable present.'

When they were alone, Rosalind's conversation was still full of Orlando. Celia began to realize that her cousin had fallen in love with the handsome young wrestler and she said to Rosalind, 'Is it possible you could fall in love so suddenly?'

Rosalind replied, 'The duke, my father, loved his father dearly.'

'But,' Celia said, 'does it follow that you should love his son dearly? Then I ought to hate him, for my father hated his father, but I do not hate Orlando.'

Frederick was in a filthy temper after seeing Sir Rowland de Boys' son, who re-

minded him of the many friends the banished duke had. Having been displeased with his niece for some time because people praised her for her goodness and pitied her for her father's sake, his spite suddenly broke out against her. While Celia and Rosalind were chatting about Orlando, Frederick strode into the room and angrily ordered Rosalind to leave the palace instantly and follow her father into banishment. Celia begged him to let her stay but he said that he had only put up with Rosalind on her account. 'I did not then,' said Celia, 'beg you to let her stay, for I was too young at that time to value her. Now that I know her worth, and because for so long we have slept in the same room, got up at the same instant, learned, played and eaten together, I cannot live without her.'

Frederick replied, 'She is too sly for you. Her smoothness, her very silence and her patience speak to the people and they pity her. You are a fool to plead for her. When she is gone you will seem brighter and better. So do not open your mouth in her favour, for the judgement which I have passed upon her cannot be taken back.'

When Celia found she could not persuade her father to let Rosalind stay with her, she generously decided to go with her. Leaving her father's palace that night, she went along with her friend to look for Rosalind's father, the banished duke, in the Forest of Arden.

Celia thought that it would be unsafe for two young women to travel in the rich clothes they usually wore. She suggested that they should dress themselves as country girls.

Rosalind said it would be a still greater protection if one of them was dressed like a man. They agreed that, as Rosalind was the taller, she should wear boy's clothes and that Celia should be dressed like a country lass. They decided that they should say they

were brother and sister. Rosalind said she would be called Ganymede and Celia chose the name of Aliena.

In this disguise, and taking their money and jewels to pay for whatever they needed, the two girls set out on their long journey. The Forest of Arden was a long way off, beyond the boundaries of the duke's lands.

Rosalind, or Ganymede, as she must now be called, seemed to have put on manly courage with her man's clothes. She paid back the faithful friendship Celia had shown in accompanying her so many weary miles by being encouraging and cheerful, as if she were, indeed, Ganymede, the rustic and stout-hearted brother of the gentle village girl, Aliena.

When at last they reached the Forest of Arden, there were no more inns for food and lodging. Hungry and tired Ganymede now admitted to Aliena that he was so weary he could find it in his heart to disgrace his man's clothes and cry like a woman. Aliena declared she could go no further. Ganymede tried to remember that it was a man's duty to comfort and console a woman. To seem courageous to his new sister, he said, 'Come, be of good heart, my sister Aliena; we are now at the end of our journey in the Forest of Arden!' But pretend manliness and forced courage could no longer help them. Although they were in the Forest of Arden, they did not know where to find the duke. Here the journey of these weary girls might have come to a sad end, for they would probably have lost themselves and died of hunger. However, as they were sitting on the grass, almost collapsing with exhaustion and not expecting any help, a countryman came past. Ganymede once more tried to speak with manly courage, saying, 'Shepherd, can love or gold buy comfort for us in this deserted place? If so, please, take us somewhere where we can rest for this young girl, my sister, is worn out with travelling and faints from hunger.'

The man replied that he was only a servant to a shepherd and that his master's house was just going to be sold. He said they would find poor comfort but if they wanted to go with him, they would be welcome to what there was. They followed the man, the prospect of shelter giving them fresh strength. They bought the shepherd's house and sheep and asked the countryman to be their servant. So, very fortunately they were provided with a neat cottage and plenty of food. They agreed to stay there till they could learn where in the forest the duke lived.

When they were rested after the exhaustion of their journey, they began to like their new way of life. They almost believed themselves to be the shepherd and shepherdess they pretended to be. Still, sometimes, Ganymede remembered he had once been Rosa-

lind who had fallen in love with the brave Orlando because he was the son of Sir Rowland, her father's friend. Although Ganymede thought that Orlando was many miles away it soon turned out that he was in the forest, too.

When Sir Rowland de Boys died, he left him, Orlando, who was then very young, in the care of his eldest brother Oliver. He told Oliver to give his brother a good education and look after him properly. Oliver proved an unworthy brother. Disregarding the commands of his dying father, he never sent his brother to school, but kept him at home untaught and entirely neglected. However, Orlando's nature and mind were like those of his excellent father, so, even without the advantages of education, he seemed like a young man who had been raised with the utmost care. Oliver envied his handsome and dignified brother so much that, at last, he wished to destroy him. To do this, he set on people to persuade Orlando to wrestle with the duke's wrestler, who had killed so many men. It was his cruel brother's neglect of him which made Orlando say he wished to die.

When, in spite of his wicked hopes, Orlando won the wrestling, Oliver's jealousy and spite knew no bounds and he swore he would burn the room where Orlando slept.

An old and faithful servant, called Adam, overheard him. Adam loved Orlando because he resembled Sir Rowland, so he went out to meet him on his way back from the duke's palace. When he saw Orlando, the danger his dear young master was in made him break out into these exclamations: 'O my gentle master, my sweet master! O you memory of old Sir Rowland! Why are you good? Why are you gentle, strong, and brave? And why did you want to beat the duke's wrestler? Your praise has come too fast to our home before you.'

Orlando, wondering what all this meant, asked him what was the matter. Then old Adam told him how his wicked brother, jealous of the love all people bore him and now hearing the fame he had gained by his victory in the duke's palace, intended to kill him by setting fire to his room that night. He ended by advising him to run away immediately. Knowing that Orlando had no money, Adam had brought his savings with him. He said, 'I have five hundred crowns, money that I saved when I worked for your father and intended to use for my keep when I become too old to work. Take that and God who feeds the ravens will comfort my age! Here is the gold. I give it all to you but let me be your servant. Although I look old I will do the work of a younger man for you.'

'O good old man,' Orlando said, 'how fine your old fashioned values are! You are not made for the ways of these days. We will go along together and before your savings have been spent, I shall come upon some way of supporting us.'

Together, then, this faithful servant and his loved master set out. Orlando and Adam travelled on, unsure where to go till they came to the Forest of Arden. There they found themselves in the same terrible state of hunger as Ganymede and Aliena had been. They wandered on, looking for someone to help, till they were almost dead with hunger and tiredness. Adam said, 'O my dear master, I die for lack of food; I can go no farther!' He lay down, thinking that place would be his grave, and said goodbye to Orlando. Orlando, seeing him in this weak state, lifted up his old servant in his arms and carried him under the shelter of some pleasant trees. He said to him, 'Cheer up, dear Adam, rest your weary legs here a little while and do not talk of dying!'

Orlando then went off in search of food and, by chance, arrived at that part of the forest where the duke and his friends were just going to eat their dinner. The duke was seated on the grass under a shady canopy of trees.

Orlando was desperate and drew his sword, intending to take their meal by force. He said, 'Stop and eat no more; I must have your food!' The duke asked him if he had become so bold through troubles or if he were simply a rude person who took no notice of good manners? Orlando said he was dying of hunger, so the duke replied that he was welcome to sit down and eat with them. Orlando, hearing him speak so gently, put away his sword and blushed with shame at the rude way he had demanded their food. 'Pardon me, please,' he said. 'I thought that there were only wild things here, and therefore I put on a stern expression. Whoever you are, who live in this deserted place, under the shade of the trees, if you have known better days, if you have ever been where bells call you to church, if you have ever sat at any good man's feast, if you have ever wiped a tear from your eyelids and known what it is to pity or to be pitied, may polite words now move you to be kind to me?'

The duke replied, 'It is true that we are men who have seen better days, and though we now live in this wild forest, we have lived in towns and cities, and have been called to church by the sound of holy bells, have sat at good men's feasts, have wiped tears of pity from our eyes. So sit down and take as much food as you want.'

'There is an old poor man,' Orlando answered, 'who has limped after me many a weary step out of pure love. He suffers in two ways at the same time: through age and hunger. Until he has had enough to eat I must not touch a bit.'

'Go, find him and bring him here,' said the duke, 'we won't eat till you return.'

Then Orlando went like a doe to find its fawn and give it food. He soon returned, carrying Adam in his arms and the duke said, 'Set down your good servant. You are both welcome.' They fed the old man and cheered his heart. He revived and recovered his health and strength again.

The duke asked who Orlando was. When he found that he was the son of his old friend, Sir Rowland de Boys, he took him under his protection and Orlando and Adam lived with the duke in the forest.

All this happened quite soon after Ganymede and Aliena bought the shepherd's cottage. They were strangely surprised to find the name Rosalind carved on the trees and love poems fastened to them, all addressed to Rosalind. While they were wondering what this was all about, they met Orlando, and they noticed that he wore the chain which Rosalind had given him around his neck.

Orlando little thought that Ganymede was the very woman who had so won his heart that he passed his whole time in carving her name on the trees and writing poems in praise of her beauty. Still, he liked the young shepherd and started talking to him. Ganymede played the role of a young man halfway between boyhood and manhood. With humour he talked to Orlando of a certain lover, 'who,' he said, 'haunts our forest and spoils our young trees with carving "Rosalind" on their barks. He hangs poems upon hawthorns and rhymes upon brambles, all praising this same Rosalind. If I could

find this lover, I would give him some good advice that would soon cure him of his love.'

Orlando admitted that he was the lover who wrote the poems and asked Ganymede to give him the good advice he had mentioned. The cure Ganymede suggested was that Orlando should come every day to the cottage where he and his sister Aliena lived. 'And then,' said Ganymede, 'I will pretend to be Rosalind and you will pretend to say loving things to me just as you do if I really were Rosalind. Then I will imitate the silly ways women behave to their lovers till I make you ashamed of your love. This is the way to cure you.'

Orlando had no great faith in the cure, but he agreed to come every day to Ganymede's cottage and pretend to talk to Rosalind. Every day Orlando visited Ganymede and Aliena and Orlando called the shepherd his Rosalind. Every day he said all fine words and flattering compliments which young men like to use to the young women they love.

Orlando thought this was all a game, not dreaming that Ganymede really was Rosalind. Nevertheless, the opportunity it gave him of saying all the fond things he had in his heart pleased him almost as much as it did Ganymede, who enjoyed the secret joke in knowing that these fine love speeches were all addressed to the right person.

The days passed pleasantly. The good-natured Aliena, seeing it made Ganymede happy, let him have his own way and enjoyed the mock courtship. She did not care to remind Ganymede that Rosalind had not yet made herself known to her father, although they had learned from Orlando where he lived. Ganymede met the duke one day and had a talk with him. The duke asked what a family he came from. Ganymede answered that he came of as good family as he did. This made the duke smile, for he did not suspect the shepherd boy came from a royal family. Seeing the duke look well and happy, Ganymede was content to put off all further explanation for a few days longer.

One morning, as Orlando was going to visit Ganymede, he saw a man lying asleep on the ground. A large green snake had twisted about his neck. The snake, seeing Orlando approach, glided away among the bushes. Orlando went nearer and discovered a lioness crouching, with her head on the ground, watching like a cat. She was waiting till the sleeping man woke, for it is said that lions will prey on nothing that is dead or sleeping. It seemed that Orlando had been sent to save the man from the danger of the snake and lioness. When Orlando looked at the man's face, he recognized his own brother Oliver. He had so cruelly mistreated him, and had threatened to kill him by fire, that Orlando was almost tempted to leave him to the hungry lioness. Brotherly affection and the gentleness of his nature soon overcame his first anger against his brother, so he drew his sword and attacked the lioness. He killed her and so saved his brother's life twice — from the poisonous snake and the furious lioness. However, Orlando had been clawed by the lioness in the fight.

While Orlando was fighting the lioness, Oliver had woken up and realized that his brother was saving him from the fury of a wild beast at the risk of his own life. He was overcome with shame and remorse and was sorry that he had treated Orlando so badly. With many tears he begged his brother's pardon. Orlando was glad that Oliver was sorry and readily forgave him. They hugged each other. From that hour Oliver loved Orlando like a proper brother.

The wound in Orlando's arm was bleeding and he felt too weak to visit Ganymede. He asked his brother to go and tell Ganymede 'who,' said Orlando, 'I call my Rosalind as a sort of joke,' of the accident which had happened to him.

Oliver went there and told to Ganymede and Aliena how Orlando saved his life. When he had finished the story of Orlando's bravery and his own escape, he admitted to them that he was Orlando's brother, who had been so cruel to him. Then he told them about how he and Orlando had now become friends.

Oliver's real sadness for his offences made such a strong impression on Aliena's kind heart that she instantly fell in love with him. Oliver, noticing how much she pitied his distress over his faults, just as suddenly fell in love with her. While love was stealing into the hearts of Oliver and Aliena, it was no less busy with Ganymede. Hearing of the danger Orlando had been in and that he was wounded by the lioness, he fainted. When he recovered, he claimed that he had pretended to faint in the character of Rosalind. Ganymede said to Oliver, 'Tell your brother Orlando how well I pretended to faint.' Oliver saw by the paleness of his face that he really had fainted and wondering at the weakness of the young man, he said, 'Well, if you did pretend, take good heart and pretend to be a man.'

'That's what I do,' replied Ganymede, truly, 'but I should have been a woman by right.'

Oliver made this visit a very long one. When he at last returned to his brother, he had lots of news to tell him. Apart from the story of Ganymede's fainting at hearing that Orlando was wounded, Oliver told him how he had fallen in love with the pretty shepherdess Aliena and that she had been encouraging. He told his brother that he was going to marry Aliena, saying that he loved her so much that he would live in the forest as a shepherd and give his lands and house to Orlando.

'I agree,' said Orlando. 'Let's have your wedding tomorrow and I will invite the duke and his friends. Go and persuade your shepherdess to agree to this. She is alone at the moment, for look, here comes her brother.' Oliver went off to see Aliena.

Orlando and Ganymede began to talk over the sudden love which had struck both Oliver and Aliena. Orlando said that he had advised his brother to persuade his pretty shepherdess to be married the next day. He added how much he wished he could be married on the same day to his Rosalind.

Ganymede, who approved of this arrangement, said that if Orlando really loved Rosalind as much as he said he did, he should have his wish. He would see to it that Rosalind would appear the next day and also that she would be willing to marry Orlando.

Ganymede pretended he would make this happen by magic, which he said, he had learned from his uncle who was a famous magician.

Orlando, half believing and half doubting what he heard, asked Ganymede if he really meant it.

'By my life I do,' said Ganymede. 'So put on your best clothes and ask the duke and your friends to your wedding. If you want to be married to Rosalind tomorrow, she shall be here.'

Next morning, Oliver having obtained Aliena's agreement, they went to see the

duke. Orlando went with them. They were all assembled to celebrate this double marriage, but only one of the brides was there. There was a lot of wondering and guessing,
but they mostly thought that Ganymede was making fun of Orlando.

The duke, hearing that it was his own daughter who was to be brought in this strange
way, asked Orlando if he believed the shepherd boy could really do what he had promised. While Orlando was answering that he didn't know what to think, Ganymede
came in. He asked the duke whether he would agree to Rosalind's marriage with Orlando if he brought her there. 'I would,' said the duke, 'even if I had kingdoms to give with
her.'

Ganymede then said to Orlando, 'And you say you will marry her if I bring her here?'

'I will,' said Orlando, 'even if I were the king of many kingdoms.'

Ganymede and Aliena then went out together. He stripped off his male clothes and once more dressed in woman's clothes, quickly became Rosalind, without the power of magic. Aliena, changing her country dress for her own rich clothes, was, with a little trouble, transformed into Celia.

While they were gone, the duke said to Orlando that the shepherd Ganymede reminded him of his daughter Rosalind. Orlando said that he also had noticed the resemblance.

They had no time to wonder how all this would end, for Rosalind and Celia, dressed in their own clothes, came in. No longer pretending that it was by the power of magic that she came there, Rosalind threw herself on her knees before her father and begged his blessing. It seemed so wonderful to everybody who was there that she should appear so suddenly that it might well have passed for magic. Rosalind told her father the story of her banishment and of her living in the forest as a shepherd boy, with her cousin Celia passing as her sister.

The duke once more agreed to the marriage and Orlando and Rosalind, Oliver and Celia were married at the same time. Although their wedding could not be celebrated with any of the splendour usual on such occasions, a happier wedding-day was never passed. While they were eating their meal under the cool shade of the pleasant trees, as if nothing could make the good duke and the true lovers any happier, an unexpected messenger arrived to tell the duke the joyful news that his dukedom had been restored to him.

Duke Frederick, enraged that Celia had run away, hearing that every day good men joined the lawful duke in his exile in the Forest of Arden, and jealous that his brother should be highly respected even in his hard circumstances, put himself at the head of a large army. They set out towards the forest, intending to seize the duke and kill him and all his faithful followers, but, just as he entered the outskirts of the forest, he met an old religious man, a hermit. They talked for a long time and in the end the hermit completely turned his heart from his wicked plan. He was truly sorry and decided to give up his unjust dukedom and spend the rest of his life in a monastery. The first thing he did to show he was sorry was to send a messenger to his brother to offer to restore his dukedom together with the lands and money of his friends.

This joyful news, as unexpected as it was welcome, came just at the right moment to heighten the festivity and rejoicing at the weddings. Celia complimented her cousin on the good fortune which had happened to the duke, Rosalind's father, and wished her joy, although she herself was no longer heir to the dukedom. For now that her father had his dukedom back, Rosalind was the heir, but the two cousins loved each other and never felt any jealousy.

The duke was able to reward his true friends who had stayed with him in his banishment. Although they had patiently shared his bad luck, they were very pleased to return in peace and prosperity to the palace of their lawful duke.

The Merchant of Venice

Shylock the Jew lived in Venice. He was a money-lender, who had got an immense fortune from lending money at a high rate of interest to Christian merchants. Interest is an extra payment for being allowed to borrow money. Shylock, being a hard-hearted man, insisted on the repayment of the money he lent with such severity that he was much disliked by all good men, particularly by Antonio, a merchant of Venice. Shylock hated Antonio because he used to lend money to people in trouble and never took any interest for his loan. Whenever Antonio met Shylock on the Rialto Bridge, he used to tell him off for being so mean and hard. Shylock would pretend to be patient about this but he secretly planned revenge.

Antonio was the kindest man and never grew tired of helping others. Indeed, he showed ancient Roman honour more than anyone else in Italy. He was liked very much by all his fellow citizens, but his best friend was Bassanio, a noble Venetian. He had inherited a small amount of money from his father but he had spent nearly all of it by living too extravagantly as young men of high rank and little money is too apt to do. Whenever Bassanio wanted money, Antonio helped him and it seemed as if they had but one heart and one purse between them.

One day Bassanio came to Antonio and told him that he wished to marry a rich woman, whose father had recently died and left her sole heiress to a large estate. In her father's lifetime he used to visit her house and had fallen in love with her. He thought she had sometimes sent him silent signals with eyes that seemed to say she liked him, too. Having no money to dress himself properly as the lover of so rich an heiress, he asked Antonio to add to the many favours he had already shown him by lending him three thousand ducats.

Antonio had no money available at that time to lend his friend. However, he was expecting some ships to come home full of rich cargo soon. So he said he would go to Shylock, the rich money-lender, and borrow the money upon the credit of those ships.

Antonio and Bassanio went to Shylock together and Antonio asked him to lend him three thousand ducats upon any interest he should require to be paid out of the cargo contained in his ships at sea. Shylock thought to himself, 'If I can catch him out, I will get my own back. He hates our Jewish nation; he lends out money without any charge and tells me off in front of the others and criticizes my well-earned bargains, which he calls interest. Cursed be my tribe if I forgive him!'

Antonio finding that Shylock was thinking something out and did not answer, and being impatient for the money, said, 'Shylock, do you hear? Will you lend the money?'

To this question Shylock replied, 'Signior Antonio, on the Rialto you have often complained about my money and my money-lending, and I have put up with it with a patient shrug, for suffering is the badge of all Jews. Then you called me unbeliever, cut-throat dog, spat about my Jewish clothes and kicked as if I were a stray dog. Well, then, it now appears you need my help and you come to me and say, "Shylock, lend me money." Has a dog money? Is it possible a stray dog could lend three thousand ducats? Shall I bow down and say, "Kind sir, you spat upon me on Wednesday last, another time you called me a dog, and for this politeness I am to lend you money?" '

Antonio replied, 'I am just as likely to call you a dog again, to spit on you again and kick you too. If you will lend me this money, do not lend it to me as to a friend, but rather lend it to me as to an enemy. That way if I break my promise to repay on time, you may with better face claim the fee.'

'Why, look,' said Shylock, 'at how you storm! I would like to be friends with you. I will forget the shame you have put on me. I will supply your wants and take no interest for my money.' This apparently kind offer surprised Antonio. Then Shylock, still pretending to be kind and that all he did was to gain Antonio's friendship, said again he would lend him the three thousand ducats and take no interest for his money. Antonio should go with him to a lawyer and sign as a piece of fun a bond, that said that if he did not repay the money by a certain day, he would forfeit a pound of flesh, to be cut off from any part of his body that Shylock pleased.

'All right,' Antonio said. 'I will sign this bond and say there is much kindness in you.'

Bassanio told Antonio not to sign such a bond for him but Antonio insisted that he would, for long before the day of payment was due, his ships would return with many times the value of the money.

Shylock, hearing this debate, exclaimed, 'O father Abraham, what suspicious people these Christians are! Their own hard dealings teach them to suspect the thoughts of others. Please tell me this, Bassanio: if he should break his promised day for repayment, what should I gain by demanding such a price? A pound of man's flesh is not so useful or profitable as the flesh of mutton or beef. I say, to buy his liking, I offer this friendship. If he will take it, good. If not, goodbye.

At last, against Bassanio's advice, who, regardless of everything Shylock had said of his kind intentions, did not want his friend to run the risk of this shocking penalty for his sake, Antonio signed the bond, thinking it really was just for fun.

The rich heiress that Bassanio wanted to marry lived quite near Venice at a place called Belmont. Her name was Portia, and she was just as beautiful and clever as the famous Portia, who was Cato's daughter and the wife of Brutus.

Bassanio, being so kindly supplied with money by his friend Antonio at the risk of his life, set out for Belmont with splendid attendants, and a friend called Gratiano.

Bassanio was successful and Portia soon agreed to marry him. He admitted to Portia that he had little money, and that his good family and their fine reputation were all he could boast. She loved him for his good character and had riches enough not to worry about wealth in a husband. She answered with graceful modesty that she would wish herself a thousand times more beautiful and ten thousand times richer just to be worthy of him. Then Portia charmingly criticized herself, saying that she was an uneducated girl, unpractised in life, yet not so old that she could not learn. She would commit her gentle spirit to be directed and governed by him in all things. She said, 'Myself and what is mine is now yours. Only yesterday, Bassanio, I was the mistress of this house, in

charge of myself and these servants. Now this house, these servants and myself are yours, my lord; I give them with this ring.' She presented a ring to Bassanio.

Bassanio was overwhelmed with gratitude and wonder at the way Portia, who was rich and from a noble family, accepted him. He could not find words to describe his joy and affection for this lovable lady who honoured him so greatly. He spoke many stuttering words of love and thankfulness. Taking the ring, he promised never to part with it.

Gratiano and Nerissa, Portia's lady-in-waiting, were there looking after their lord and lady, when Portia so gracefully promised to become the obedient wife of Bassanio. Gratiano, wishing Bassanio and his bride joy, asked to be allowed to be married at the same time.

'Certainly, Gratiano,' said Bassanio, 'if you can find a wife.'

Gratiano then said that he loved Portia's pretty lady-in-waiting, Nerissa, and that she had promised to marry him if Portia married Bassanio. Portia asked Nerissa if this was true. Nerissa replied, 'Madam, yes, if you don't mind.' Portia willingly agreed and Bassanio said, 'Then we can share our wedding day, Gratiano.'

The happiness of these two couples was sadly spoilt at this moment by a messenger, who brought a letter with fearful news from Antonio. When Bassanio read Antonio's letter, Portia thought it must be telling him of a dear friend's death because he looked so pale. She asked him what was wrong; he said, 'O my darling Portia, here are a few of the nastiest words that ever blotted paper. When I first told you I loved you, I freely admitted that I had no money. I should have told you that I have less than nothing because I am in debt.' Bassanio then told Portia about how he had borrowed money from Antonio, who had himself borrowed it from Shylock. He told her how Antonio had signed a bond which meant that he had to give Shylock a pound of his own flesh, if the money was not repaid by a particular day. Then Bassanio read Antonio's letter: 'Dear Bassanio, my ships are all lost at sea, my bond to Shylock must be paid. As paying it will kill me, I want to see you before my death. However, if your feelings of friendship are not enough to make you come, do not be forced by my letter.' 'O my dear love,' said Portia, 'stop everything and go. You shall have plenty of gold to pay the money twenty times over before this kind friend shall lose a hair through your fault.' Portia then said she would be married to Bassanio before he set out for Venice to give him a legal right to her money. That same day they were married. Gratiano also married Nerissa. Immediately Bassanio and Gratiano were married, they set out in a terrific hurry for Venice. There, Bassanio found Antonio in prison.

The day of repayment was actually past and cruel Shylock would not accept the money that Bassanio offered him, but insisted on having a pound of Antonio's flesh. A day was arranged to try this shocking case before the Duke of Venice. Bassanio waited full of worry.

When Bassanio left Portia, she had spoken cheerfully to him and asked him to bring his dear friend back with him when he returned. However, she was worried that things would go wrong. When she was left alone, she began to think and wondered whether she could be able to help save the life of her dear Bassanio's friend. Although she had said to Bassanio, in a meek and submissive way, that she would always agree to be ruled she now began to think hard about how she could use her abilities to save his friend from danger. She decided to go to Venice and speak in Antonio's defence.

Portia had a relation who was a lawyer. His name was Bellario. She wrote to him telling him all about the case and asking his opinion. She also asked him to send her the clothes worn by lawyers in court. When the messenger returned, he brought letters of advice about how to proceed and also everything necessary for her to wear.

Portia and Nerissa dressed in men's clothes. Putting on the robes of a lawyer, Portia took Nerissa with her as her clerk. They set out immediately and arrived in Venice on the very day of the trial. The case was just going to be heard before the duke and senators in the senate-house, when Portia entered this high court of justice. She presented a letter from Bellario, in which he wrote that he would come himself to plead for Anto-

nio, but was prevented by illness. He asked that the young Doctor Balthasar might be allowed to plead instead. Balthasar was, of course, really Portia. The duke agreed.

This important trial now began. Portia looked around and saw the merciless money lender. She saw Bassanio too, but he didn't recognize her in her disguise. He was standing beside Antonio in an agony of worry and fear for his friend.

The importance of the hard task Portia had set herself gave her courage. She started boldly in the duty she had undertaken to perform. First of all, she spoke to Shylock. She agreed that he had a right by Venetian law to have the punishment written in the bond. She spoke sweetly of the value of mercy and would have softened any heart but the unfeeling Shylock. She said that mercy dropped like gentle rain straight from heaven and that mercy was a double blessing — it blessed whoever gave and whoever received. She spoke of how mercy was a better thing for kings to have than their crowns because it is a quality of God Himself and said that earthly power came nearest to God's when strong people could forgive others instead of looking for punishment. She told Shylock to remember that we all pray for God's mercy, so that same prayer should teach us to show mercy. Shylock answered her by repeating that he wanted the penalty in the bond. 'Is he not able to pay the money?' asked Portia.

Bassanio offered Shylock the payment of the three thousand ducats as many times over as he could want. Shylock refused and still insisted upon having a pound of Antonio's flesh. Bassanio begged the learned young lawyer to try to twist the law a little to save Antonio's life. Portia answered gravely that laws, once established, must never be altered. Shylock, hearing Portia say that the law could not be altered, thought that she was on his side and he said, 'A wise man is come to judgement! A wise young judge, how I do honour you! How much older you are than you look!'

Portia now asked Shylock to let her look at the bond and when she had read it, she said, 'This bond is legal and because the money has not been paid on time, Shylock may lawfully claim a pound of flesh to be cut off by him at the place nearest Antonio's heart.' Then she said to Shylock, 'Be merciful. Take the money and let me tear up the bond.'

However, the cruel Shylock would not show any mercy. He said, 'By my soul, I swear there is no power in the tongue of man to alter me.'

'Why, then, Antonio,' said Portia, 'you must prepare your chest for the knife.' While Shylock was eagerly sharpening a long knife to cut off the pound of flesh, Portia said to Antonio. 'Have you anything to say?' With calm resignation Antonio replied that he had little to say because he had prepared his mind for death. Then he said to Bassanio, 'Shake hands, Bassanio. Goodbye. Do not grieve that I have had this bad luck because of you. Give my best wishes to your wife and tell her how good a friend I have been!'

Bassanio in total misery replied, 'Antonio, I am married to a woman I love as much as I love life itself. But life itself, my wife and all the world do not mean as much to me as your life. I would lose all; I would sacrifice everything to this devil here, to save you.'

Portia heard this and was not really offended when her husband expressed his affection to such a true a friend as Antonio in these strong words, yet she could not help answering, 'If your wife were here, she would not be very pleased to hear you make this offer.' Then Gratiano, who loved to copy what Bassanio did, thought he must make a similar speech and he said, 'I have a wife whom I love. I wish she were dead and in heaven so that she could beg some power there to change the cruel temper of this currish money lender.' 'It is a good thing you wish behind her back, or you would be in trouble,' said Nerissa, who, still dressed as a clerk, was sitting beside Portia, taking notes.

Shylock now shouted impatiently, 'We are wasting time. Please pronounce the sentence.' Everyone in the court was silent and every heart was full of sadness for Antonio.

Portia asked if the scales were ready to weigh the flesh and she said to Shylock, 'Shylock, you must have a doctor standing by in case he bleeds to death.

Shylock, whose whole intent was that Antonio *should* bleed to death, said, 'It is not written in the bond.'

Portia replied, 'So what? It would be good and kind to have a doctor here.'

All Shylock would answer was, 'I cannot find it; it is not in the bond.'

'Then,' said Portia, 'a pound of Antonio's flesh is yours. The law allows it and the court awards it. You may cut this flesh from his chest. The law allows it and the court awards it.' Again Shylock exclaimed, 'O wise and upright judge!' Then he sharpened his long knife again and looking eagerly at Antonio, he said, 'Come on, get ready!'

'Wait a moment,' said Portia, 'there is something else. This bond here does not give you one drop of blood. The express words are, "a pound of flesh". If, when you cut off the pound of flesh, you shed one drop of Antonio's blood, your land and possessions will be taken away from you. This is the law.' It was utterly impossible for Shylock to cut off a pound of flesh without shedding some of Antonio's blood, so this clever discovery of Portia's — that flesh but no blood was written in the bond — saved Antonio's life. Everyone was impressed with the wonderful cleverness of the young lawyer, who had so happily thought of this solution. Praises resounded from every corner of the senate-house and Gratiano exclaimed, in the words which Shylock had used, 'O wise and upright judge!'

Shylock, finding himself defeated, said, with a disappointed look, that he would take the money. Bassanio, delighted beyond belief at Antonio's unexpected safety, called out, 'Here is the money!'

Portia stopped him, saying, 'Just a minute. There is no hurry. Shylock shall have nothing but the penalty. So, Shylock, get ready to cut off the flesh, but mind you do not shed any blood. Also do not cut off more or less than exactly a pound. If it is more or less by so much as a scatter, if the scale fails to balance by the weight of a single hair, you are condemned by the law of Venice to die and all your money will then belong to the senate.'

'Give me my money, and let me go,' said Shylock.

'I have it ready,' said Bassanio, 'here it is.'

Shylock was going to take the money, when Portia stopped him again, saying, 'Wait! I have still another hold upon you. By the laws of Venice, your money belongs to the state because you tried to kill one of its citizens and your life depends on the mercy of the duke. Get down on your knees and ask him to pardon you.'

The duke then said to Shylock, 'You may now see the difference in our attitudes. I will let you keep your life before you ask me, but half your money belongs to Antonio, the other half comes to the state.'

Generous Antonio said that he would give up his share of Shylock's money, if Shylock would sign a legal form to give it to his daughter and her husband when he died. Antonio knew that Shylock had a daughter who had recently married a young man

called Lorenzo, against Shylock's wishes. Lorenzo was Antonio's friend. Shylock had been so angry with his daughter that he had disinherited her.

The money lender agreed to this. He was disappointed in his revenge and had lost his riches. He said, 'I am ill. Let me go home. Send the form to me and I will sign over half my riches to my daughter.'

'Go away, then,' said the duke, 'and sign it.'

The duke now released Antonio and dismissed the court. He praised the wisdom and cleverness of the young lawyer and invited him home to dinner.

Portia, who intended to get back to Belmont before her husband, replied, 'Thank you, your grace, but I must go away at once.'

The duke said he was sorry the young lawyer did not have time to stay and dine with him. Turning to Antonio, he added, 'Reward this gentleman, for, in my mind, you owe him a lot.'

The duke and his senators left the court and then Bassanio said to Portia, 'Well done, sir! My friend Antonio and I have, by your wisdom, been helped out of terrible difficulties today, and I ask you to accept the three thousand ducats that were due to be paid to Shylock.'

'And we shall still be in your debt for the rest of our lives,' said Antonio.

Portia could not be persuaded to accept the money. Bassanio still insisted that she should accept some reward, so she said, 'Give me your gloves. I will wear them to remember you by.' Then Bassanio took off his gloves and she saw the ring which she had given him upon his finger. Now it was really the ring that Portia wanted to get from him to make fun of Bassanio when she saw him again. That was what made her ask him for his gloves. She said, 'And for your thanks I will take this ring from you.'

Bassanio was very upset that the lawyer should ask him for the only thing he could not part with. He replied, in great confusion, that he could not give away this particular ring, because it was his wife's gift and he had promised never to part with it. However, he would give the lawyer the most valuable ring in Venice. On hearing this Portia pretended to be very put out and left the court, saying, 'You teach me, sir, how a beggar should be answered.'

'Dear Bassanio,' said Antonio, 'let him have the ring. Let my great friendship and the great help he has given me be valued against your wife's being cross.' Bassanio, ashamed to appear so ungrateful, gave in and sent Gratiano after Portia with the ring. Then the 'clerk' Nerissa, who had also given Gratiano a ring when she married him, asked him for his ring. Gratiano, not choosing to be outdone in generosity by Bassanio, gave it to her. The two women laughed to think how when they got home, they could complain to their husbands giving away their rings and tell them off for giving them away as presents to other women.

Portia, when she returned, was feeling very pleased with herself because she knew that she had done a good thing. She felt happy about everything she saw. The moon had never seemed to shine so brightly before and when the moon was hidden behind a cloud, then a light shining from her house at Belmont pleased her just as much. She said to Nerissa, 'That light we see is shining in my hall. How far that little candle spreads its beams! It shines just like a good action in a bad world.' Hearing the sound of music from her house, she said, 'I think that music sounds much sweeter than it does in day-time.'

Portia and Nerissa went into the house and dressed in their own clothes. They did not have to wait long for their husbands to come home. Bassanio brought Antonio with him and introduced his best friend to Portia. She had hardly finished welcoming him and congratulating him on his escape from death, when they heard Nerissa and her husband quarrelling in a corner of the room. 'A quarrel already?' said Portia. 'What is the matter?'

Gratiano replied, 'Madam, it is about a worthless ring that Nerissa gave me. The words engraved on it were *Love me and leave me not.*'

'What do the words or the value of the ring matter?' said Nerissa. 'You promised me, when I gave it to you, that you would keep it all your life. Now you say you gave it to the lawyer's clerk. I know you gave it to a woman.'

'Heavens!' replied Gratiano, 'I gave it to a young man, a kind of boy, a little scrubbed boy no taller than you are. He was clerk to the young lawyer whose wise arguments saved Antonio's life. This foolish boy asked for it as payment and I could not refuse him.'

Portia said, 'You were to blame, Gratiano, to part with your wife's first gift. I gave Bassanio a ring and I am sure he would not part with it for all the world.'

Gratiano, in excuse for his fault, now said, 'My Lord Bassanio gave his ring to the lawyer and then the boy, his clerk who worked hard writing notes, asked for my ring.'

On hearing this, Portia pretended to be very angry and told Bassanio off for giving away her ring. She said that Nerissa had taught her what to believe. Some woman had been given the ring.

Bassanio was very unhappy to have upset her so much. He said with great earnest-

ness, 'No, truly I didn't give it to another woman, I gave it to the lawyer who had already refused three thousand ducats and who asked for the ring. When I refused to give it to him, he was quite put out and went away. What could I do, darling Portia? I was so ashamed to seem ungrateful that I was forced to send the ring after him. Forgive me, but I am sure that if you had been there you would have asked me for the ring to give the worthy lawyer.'

'Ah!' said Antonio, 'I am the unhappy cause of these quarrels.'

Portia told Antonio not to upset himself over that and said that he was welcome in any case.

Then Antonio said, 'Once before I loaned my body for Bassanio's sake and if it weren't for the lawyer your husband gave the ring to, I should now be dead. I dare make another bond with my soul as the payment that your husband will never break his promise to you again.'

'Then you shall be his guarantee,' said Portia. 'Give him this ring and tell him to keep it better than the other.'

When Bassanio looked at the ring Portia had handed him, he was surprised to find it was the same one he had given away. Then Portia told him how she was the young lawyer and Nerissa was her clerk. Bassanio was amazed and delighted to realize that it was his wife's splendid courage and wisdom that had saved Antonio's life.

Then Portia welcomed Antonio again and gave him some letters, which by chance had fallen into her hands. These contained news of how Antonio's ships, which were supposed to be lost at sea, had safely arrived in harbour. So the tragic beginnings of this rich merchant's story were all forgotten in the unexpected good luck which followed. There was time to laugh at the comic adventure of the rings and the husbands who did not recognize their own wives. Gratiano happily promised in a sort of rhyming speech that

— *while he lived, he'd fear no other thing*
So sore, as keeping safe Nerissa's ring.

King Lear

Lear, King of Britain, had three daughters — Goneril, who was married to the Duke of Albany, Regan, wife of the Duke of Cornwall, and Cordelia, who was not married. Both the King of France and the Duke of Burgundy were in love with her, and were staying at King Lear's court in the hope that one of them could persuade her to marry him.

The old king was over eighty and was worn out with age and the effort of being a king. He decided to take no further part in ruling the country but to leave this to younger people. So he called his three daughters to him to find out from their own words, which of them loved him best. Then he would divide his kingdom among them according to what each one seemed to deserve.

Goneril, the eldest, declared that she loved her father more than words could say. He was dearer to her than the light of her own eyes and dearer than life and freedom. She said a great deal more of this sort of thing, which is easy to pretend where there is no real love. The king, delighted to hear this assurance of her love from her own lips and thinking she meant what she said, gave her and her husband one-third of his kingdom.

Then he called his second daughter and demanded what she had to say. Regan, who was as unloving as her elder sister, was not a jot behind in her outpourings. She said that what her sister had said fell short of the love which she claimed to feel for the king. She said that she found all other joys dead compared with the pleasure she took in the love of her dear king and father.

Lear thought he was blessed in having such loving children. He decided he could do no less, after the splendid things Regan had said, than give a third of his kingdom to her and her husband, just as he had already given to Goneril.

Then, turning to his youngest daughter Cordelia, whom he called his joy, he asked what she had to say. No doubt he thought that she would gladden his heart with the same sort of loving speeches as her sisters. In fact he expected that her words would be much stronger than theirs, as she had always been his darling and favourite. Cordelia was disgusted with the flattery of her sisters, whose hearts she knew were far from their words. She knew that all their coaxing speeches were only intended to wheedle the old king out of his kingdom so that they and their husbands might reign in his lifetime. She said only this, that she loved her father just as much as she should — neither more nor less.

The king was shocked with what seemed like ingratitude in his favourite child. He told her to consider her words and change what she had said in case it should spoil her future.

Cordelia then told her father that he was her father, that he had given her life and loved her and that she returned those duties as was most appropriate. She obeyed him, loved him and respected him, but she could not bring herself to make such grand speeches as her sisters had or promise never to love anyone else in the world. Why had her sisters got married, if they did not love anyone except their father? If she should ever get married, she was sure her husband would want half her love and half her care and respect.

Cordelia, who truly loved her old father almost as much as her sisters pretended to do, would have plainly told him so at any other time in more daughter-like and loving words, without these qualifications. After the crafty flattering speeches of her sisters, which she had seen win such extravagant rewards, she thought the best thing she could do was to love and be silent. This would show that her love was not just because she would be given something, that it was real. She thought that making less fuss about how much she loved her father would show the truth and sincerity of her feelings.

This plainness of speech, which Lear called pride, made the old king furious. At the best of times he was a bad-tempered man and now that he had grown old, he did not think very clearly. Now, he could not tell the difference between truth and flattery, or between fine words and thoughts that came from the heart. He was so cross that instead of giving the third part of his kingdom to Cordelia, which he had intended to do, he shared it equally between her two sisters and their husbands, the Dukes of Albany and Cornwall. He then called the two dukes and, in front of all his courtiers, gave them a coronet between them. He gave them jointly all the power, money and running of the kingdom, but kept for himself the title of king. He gave up all the rest of the royal matters. His one condition was that he and a hundred knights for his attendants should live at each of his daughters' palaces in turn for a month.

This ridiculous division of his kingdom, showing so little sense and so much bad temper, filled all his courtiers with astonishment and sadness, but none of them had the courage to say anything, except the Earl of Kent. He was just beginning to speak a good word for Cordelia, when Lear, on pain of death, furiously commanded him to be

quiet. Kent was not so easily stopped. He had always been loyal to Lear, whom he had respected as a king, loved as a father and followed as a master. He had always considered his life as being at the king's service to fight against Lear's enemies. He was always prepared to lose it when Lear's safety was in danger. Now Lear was his own enemy, but this did not make such a faithful servant of the king forget his old beliefs. He bravely stood up to Lear for Lear's own good and only seemed rude because the king was mad. In the past, he had been a most faithful adviser to the king and he pleaded with Lear that he would still take his advice. He asked Lear to reconsider his angry decision and change his mind. Kent said he would bet his life that Lear's youngest daughter did not love her father least. Just because she said little, did not mean she felt little. If powerful kings believed flattery, then truthful people had to use plain words. As for Lear's threats, what could the king do to Kent whose life was already at his service? That should not prevent him from speaking the truth.

The good Earl of Kent's honest words only stirred up the king's anger more. He was like a frantic patient who kills his doctor and loves his illness. He banished this true servant, and allowed him only five days to make his preparations for departure. If, on the sixth day, he was found still in Britain, he would be put to death. Kent said goodbye to the king. Before he went he said he hoped Cordelia would be protected by the gods, as she had the right feelings and had spoken well. He wished that her sisters' grand speeches might turn into deeds of love. Then he went, as he said, to make a new life in a new country.

The King of France and the Duke of Burgundy were now called in to hear what Lear had decided about his youngest daughter. He wanted to know whether they still wanted to marry her now that she was in disgrace and had no fortune except her own nature to offer. The Duke of Burgundy said that he would not take her as his wife on such conditions. The King of France, however, understood how she had lost the love of her father. He knew that it was only her slowness in making speeches and that she could not bring herself to flatter like her sisters. He took Cordelia by the hand and said that her goodness was worth more than a kingdom. He told her to say goodbye to her sisters and her father, although he had been unkind, and that she should go with him and be queen of France. She would rule over better lands than her sisters. He called the Duke of Burgundy a waterish duke because his love for this young girl had run away like water in a moment.

Then Cordelia, in tears, said goodbye to her sisters and asked them to love their father well and make sure that all they had said came true. They sulkily told her not to tell

them what to do, for they knew their duty. They said she should concentrate on making her husband happy, as he had taken her, as they tauntingly expressed it, out of pity. Cordelia left with a heavy heart, for she knew how cunning her sisters were and she wished that her father was in better hands than theirs.

No sooner had Cordelia gone than her sisters began to show themselves in their true colours. Even before the end of the first month which Lear spent with the eldest daughter, Goneril, the old king began to find out the difference between promises and performances. Once she had got everything that he had to give from her father, even the crown from off his head, she began to begrudge even those small remains of royalty which the old man had kept to make him feel still a king. She could not bear to see him and his hundred knights. Every time she met him, she frowned and when the old man wanted to talk to her, she pretended to be ill to be rid of the sight of him. It was obvious that she thought he was a boring old nuisance and that his attendants were an unnecessary expense. Not only did she not bother with the king, but her example — and it is to be feared — her private instructions made her servants treat him with neglect. They either refused to obey his orders, or worse, pretended not to hear them. Lear could not fail to see this change in his daughter's behaviour, but he shut his eyes against it as long as he could. People are often unwilling to believe the unpleasant results of their own mistakes and obstinacy.

True love and faithfulness do not change because of bad treatment any more than lies and an empty heart can be improved by good treatment. This could be seen in the behaviour of the good Earl of Kent. Although banished by Lear and with his life in danger if he should be found in Britain, he chose to stay as long as there was a chance of being useful to the king. He disguised himself as a servant and offered his services to the king, who did not recognize him. Lear was pleased with the plain speaking of his servant, having become sick of the smooth, oily flattery of his daughter. A bargain was struck and Lear took Kent into his service. He called himself Caius and Lear never suspected him to be his once great favourite, the Earl of Kent.

Caius quickly found a way to show his faithfulness and affection to his royal master. That very day Goneril's steward behaved in a disrespectful manner to Lear, being cheeky, as he no doubt was secretely encouraged to do by his mistress. Caius could not bear to hear such insulting behaviour to the king and without delay tripped the steward and sent him away. Lear was delighted and became more and more attached to him.

Kent was not the only friend Lear had. The fool or jester, who had been at his palace when Lear was still a real king, remained with him after he had given away his crown. His witty sayings would keep up Lear's good humour, although he could not refrain sometimes from mocking his master for his silliness in uncrowning himself and giving everything to his daughters.

He had plenty of wild sayings and scraps of songs poured out of his heart even in front of Goneril herself. Many of his bitter taunts and jests cut to the quick. He compared the king to a hedge sparrow that feeds the young of the cuckoo till they grow old enough, and then has its head bitten off for its pains. He said, too, that an ass may know when the cart draws the horse, meaning that Lear's daughters, who should have gone behind, now ranked before their father. He added that Lear was no longer Lear, but the shadow of Lear. Once or twice he was threatened with a whipping for speaking so freely.

The coolness and rudeness which Lear had begun to notice were not all which this foolish, fond father was to suffer from his unworthy daughter. She now told him that his staying in her palace was inconvenient so long as he insisted on keeping a hundred knights. She said that this was useless and expensive and filled her court with riot and feasting. She asked him to get rid of them and keep only the old men such as himself, who were suitable for his age.

At first Lear could not believe his eyes and ears, nor could he believe that it was his daughter who spoke so unkindly. She had received a crown from him and now wanted to get rid of his attendants, grudging him the respect due to his old age. She continued her undutiful demand. The old man was beside himself with anger and called her a hateful monster and a liar. So she was, for Lear's knights were all well-behaved men with excellent manners, not given to rioting and feasting, as Goneril had said. He ordered his horse to be prepared, for he and his hundred knights would go to stay with his other daughter, Regan. He spoke of ingratitude and said that it was like a marble-hearted devil, and was more hideous in a child than in a sea-monster. He cursed Goneril in a way that was terrible to hear. He said he hoped that she might never have a child, but if she did, that it might live to treat her with the same scorn and contempt that she had shown

to him. Then she might feel how painful it was to have a thankless child. Goneril's husband, the Duke od Albany, began to make excuses for his part in Goneril' unkindness, but Lear would not hear him out. In a rage he ordered his horse to be saddled and set out with his followers for his other daughter's palace. Lear thought to himself how small Cordelia's wrong, if it had been a wrong, now appeared in comparison with her sisters'. His tears fell and then he was ashamed that such a creature as Goneril should be able to make him cry.

Regan and her husband were keeping their court in great pomp and state at their palace. Lear sent his servant Caius on ahead with letters to his daughter so that she might get ready for him. However, Goneril had been faster and also sent letters to Regan. She accused her father of being tiresome and bad tempered and advised her sister not to receive all the knights he was bringing with him. This messenger arrived at the same time as Caius and the two men met. Who should Goneril's messenger be but Caius's enemy, the steward, whom he had once tripped up for his cheeky behaviour to Lear? Caius not liking the fellow's look and suspecting what he came for, began to call him rude names and challenged him to fight. When the fellow refused, Caius, in a fit of honest passion, beat him soundly just as a mischief-maker and carrier of wicked messages deserved. When the news of this reached the ears of Regan and her husband, they ordered Caius to be put in the stocks, although he was the king's messenger and entitled to the highest respect. So the first thing Lear saw when he entered the castle was his faithful servant Caius sitting in that disgraceful situation.

This was a bad sign but worse followed. When he asked for his daughter and her husband, he was told they were tired with travelling all night and could not see him. Lear insisted angrily and when they finally came to greet him, who was with them but the hated Goneril. She had come to tell her own story and set her sister against the king, her father!

This sight upset the old man and he was even more to see Regan take Goneril by the hand. He asked Goneril if she was not ashamed to look upon his old white beard. Regan advised him to go home again with Goneril and live with her peaceably, with only a half of his attendants. She said that he should ask her forgiveness for he was old and didn't know his own mind. He must let people who knew better than him tell him what to do. Lear pointed out how absurd it would be if he had to go down on his knees and beg his own daughter for food and clothes. He said he would never return with her; but stay where he was with Regan. He said that she had not forgotten how he had given her half his kingdom and that her eyes were not fierce like Goneril's, but mild and kind.

Finally he added that rather than return to Goneril with only half his knights, he would go to France and ask help there from the king, who had married his youngest daughter although she had nothing.

He was mistaken in expecting kinder treatment from Regan than he had experienced from Goneril. As if wanting to outdo her sister in mean behaviour, she declared that she thought fifty knights too many; twenty-five would be enough. Lear, nearly broken-hearted, turned to Goneril and said that he would go back with her, for her fifty doubled twenty-five, so her love was twice as much as Regan's. Goneril excused herself and said, 'What do you need so many as twenty-five for? Or even ten? Or five? You can be waited on by my servants, or my sister's.'

So these two wicked daughters, as if they were trying to outdo each other in cruelty to their old father who had been so good to them, would have gradually deprived him of all his knights and everything that was left to show that he had once been a king! Not that a hundred knights are essential to happiness but from king to beggar is a hard change; it is strange to go from commanding millions to being without a single attendant. It was the ingratitude of his daughters' refuting him more than the difficulty of being without his knights which pierced this poor king to the heart. What with this double unkindness and annoyance with himself for so foolishly having given away a kingdom, his mind began to become unsettled. Without really knowing what he was saying, he promised revenge on those unnatural witches and to make examples of them that should be a terror to the earth!

While he was making threats that he would never be able to carry out, night came on and a loud thunderstorm began. Rain poured down, but his daughters still refused to admit his knights. He called for his horse and chose to stay out in the appalling weather rather than stay under the same roof as these ungrateful daughters. They, saying that the harm which wilful men bring on themselves is a fair punishment, let him go and shut their doors.

The wind roared and the storm raged, as the old man set off. There was scarcely even a bush for miles. Exposed to the fury of the storm in a dark night, King Lear wandered out on to the heath. He shouted at the winds to throw the earth into the sea or make the waves swell up till they drowned the earth, so that no sign might remain of such an ungrateful animal as man. The old king was now left with only the poor fool. He still made jokes and sharp comments, saying it was a naughty night to swim in and that the king had better go in and ask his daughters' blessing.

But he that has a little tiny wit,
With heigh ho, the wind and the rain!
Must make content with his fortunes fit,
Though the rain it raineth every day.

He said it was a good night for cooling a lady's pride.

This once great king, with just his jester for companionship, was finally found by his ever-faithful servant, the good Earl of Kent. He was still disguised as Caius and the king still did not recognize him as the earl. Caius said, 'Goodness, sir, what are you here? Even creatures that love the night, do not love such nights as these. This dreadful storm has driven even the animals to their hiding-places. Nobody could bear the misery or the fear.'

Lear told him off and said that these smaller problems could not be felt when someone was suffering from something much worse. When mind is at ease, the body has time to be sensitive. However, he was so disturbed and miserable about what happened to him that he was not even aware of anything else. He spoke of the ingratitude of his daughters and said it was just as if a mouth bit the hand for lifting food to it; for parents were hands and food and everything to children.

Caius, still pleading with the king not to stay out in the open air, at last persuaded him to enter a wretched little hut. The fool went in first and suddenly ran back out, terrified, saying that he had seen a spirit. On investigation this spirit proved to be nothing more than a poor mad beggar. He had crept into this deserted hut for shelter and his talk about devils had frightened the fool. He was one of those poor lunatics who are either really mad or pretend to be in order to get charity from kind country people. They go about the country calling themselves Poor Tom and Poor Turlygood, saying, 'Who gives anything to Poor Tom?' and sticking pins and nails and sprigs of rosemary into their arms to make them bleed. With these horrible acts and partly by prayers, partly with lunatic curses, they move or terrify the ignorant country folks into giving them money. This poor fellow was just such a one. The king, seeing him in such a wretched condition, with nothing but a blanket wrapped around his bare body, was convinced that the fellow was some father who had given everything away to his daughters. He thought nothing could bring a man to such wretchedness but having unkind daughters.

From this and other wild remarks Caius could plainly see that he was not in his right mind, and that his daughters' cruelty had really driven him mad. Now the loyalty of the Earl of Kent showed itself in more important ways than he had previously been able to undertake. With the help of some of the king's attendants who remained loyal, he arranged for Lear to be taken to Dover Castle, where he had many friends. Meanwhile, he sailed for France, hurrying to the court of Cordelia. He told her all about the pitiful condition of her royal father and described the inhumanity of her sisters in such detail that she cried. She asked the king, her husband, to let her leave to sail to England with enough soldiers to overcome these cruel daughters and their husbands and put the old king back on his throne. The King of France agreed and she set out with a royal army for Dover.

Lear, by some chance, had escaped from the guardians which the good Earl of Kent had put over him to take care of him in his madness. He was found wandering about the fields near Dover, by some of Cordelia's men. He was in a dreadful state, stark mad and singing aloud to himself. He had made a crown from straw, nettles and other wild weeds that he had picked in the cornfields and put it on his head. Cordelia was longing to see her father, but the doctor persuaded her to put off the meeting until sleep and herbal medicines had restored the old king. Cordelia promised the doctors all her gold and jewels if they could make Lear well again. They were so skilful that he was soon in condition to see his daughter.

It was a moving sight to see the meeting between father and daughter — to watch the struggle between the joy of this poor old king at seeing his once favourite child, and his shame at receiving such kindnesses from her after he had thrown her out for so small a fault. Both these feelings struggled with the remains of his illness, so that, in his half-crazed state, he was not always sure where he was or who it was that so kindly kissed him and spoke to him. Then he would ask the bystanders not to laugh at him if he were mistaken in thinking this lady was his daughter Cordelia. Then he fell on his knees to ask her forgiveness. She, good lady, was also kneeling to ask his blessing and was telling him that it was not right for him to kneel, but it was her duty, for she was his child, his true and very child, Cordelia! She kissed him, as she said, to kiss away all her sisters' un-kindness. She said that they should be ashamed of themselves to drive their kind old father out into the cold air, when she would have kept her enemy's dog by her fire on such a night, even though it had bitten her. She told her father how she had come from France to bring him help. He said that she must forget and forgive, for he was old and foolish and did not know what he did, but she certainly had good cause not to love him. There was no reason, however, for her sisters not to love him. Cordelia replied that she had no more cause than they.

So we will leave this old king in the protection of his dutiful and loving child. With the help of sleep and medicine, she and her doctors at last succeeded in soothing his troubled mind which the cruelty of his other daughters had so violently shaken. Let us return to say a word or two about them.

These monsters of ingratitude, who had been so false to their old father, could hardly be expected to prove more faithful to their own husbands. They soon grew tired of showing even the appearance of duty and affection. They openly fixed their loves upon another man. The object of their guilty affection was the same. His name was Edmund. He was one of the sons of the Earl of Gloucester, who had recently died. He had treacherously stolen the earldom from his brother Edgar, the lawful heir. He was a wicked man and just right for the love of such wicked creatures as Goneril and Regan. About this time, the Duke of Cornwall, Regan's husband, died. Regan immediately announced that she was going to marry this false Earl of Gloucester. This stirred up Goneril's jealousy of her sister, because Edmund had also told her that he loved her. Goneril found a way to poison her sister but was found out by her husband the Duke of Albany and put in prison. In a fit of disappointed love and rage she shortly afterwards put an end to her own life. So justice at last overtook these wicked daughters.

It was certainly fair that Goneril and Regan should come to a bad end, but, sadly, life is not always fair in all things. If it were, then Cordelia's gentleness and kindness would have been rewarded with a long and happy life, but this was not to be. The armies which Goneril and Regan had sent out under the command of the bad Earl of Gloucester were victorious against Cordelia's French soldiers. This wicked earl, who did not want anyone to stand between him and the throne, put her in prison and then had her killed. Lear, heart-broken at her death, died with his arms around her.

Before Lear died, the good Earl of Kent, who had followed him from the first of his daughters' cruel treatment to these sad last moments, tried to make him understand that he had been the servant Caius. In his misery over Cordelia, Lear could not understand how that could be or how Kent and Caius could be the same person. So Kent decided not to trouble him with any more explanations. When Lear died, soon after, this faithful friend and servant to the king soon followed him to the grave.

It is not necessary to tell how judgment finally overtook the bad Earl of Gloucester, who was killed in single combat by his brother, the lawful earl, nor how Goneril's husband, the Duke of Albany, who had never encouraged his wife in her wicked behaviour to her father, eventually became king. Lear and his three daughters, whose adventures alone concern our story, were all dead.

Macbeth

When Duncan was King of Scotland, there lived a great lord, called Macbeth. Macbeth was a close relative of the king and highly respected at court for his bravery and skill in the wars. He had recently shown his courage in defeating a huge rebel army assisted by Norwegian soldiers.

Macbeth and another Scottish general called Banquo were returning from this great battle over a bleak heath. They were stopped on their way by the strange appearance of three figures, who looked like women, except that they had beards. Their withered skins and wild clothes made them look quite unearthly. Macbeth spoke to them but they seemed to be offended. Each one placed a choppy finger upon her skinny lips as a sign to be silent. The first of them greeted Macbeth with his proper title of Thane of Glamis. He was startled to find himself known by such creatures but was even more surprised when the second weird woman called him Thane of Cawdor. He had no claim at all to this title. He was completely astonished when the third bid him, 'All hail! King that will be!' Telling the future like this might well amaze him, for he knew that while the king's sons lived he could not hope to succeed to the throne.

Turning to Banquo, these strange creatures told him, in a sort of riddle, that he would be 'lesser than Macbeth and greater! not so happy, but much happier'! They said that although he would never be a king himself, his sons would be kings of Scotland. Then the weird sisters turned into air and vanished, so the two generals knew that they had been talking to witches.

While they stood puzzling over the strangeness of this adventure, messengers from the king arrived. They had come to tell Macbeth that he had been made Thane of Cawdor. This corresponded so miraculously with the prediction of the witches that Macbeth was astonished. He stood wrapped in amazement, unable to make any reply to the messengers. Hope began to arise in his mind that the prediction of the third witch might also come true and he should one day be King of Scotland.

Turning to Banquo, he said, 'Do you hope that your children will really be kings, now that one of the things the witches promised to me has actually happened?'

'That hope,' Banquo replied, 'might encourage you to aim at the throne. Often these creatures of darkness tell us little truths to make us wicked things.'

The witches' suggestions had sunk too deep into the mind of Macbeth to let him pay

attention to Banquo's warnings. From that time, he concentrated all his thoughts on how to gain the throne of Scotland.

Macbeth told his wife about the strange prediction of the weird sisters and how it had partly come true. She was an ambitious woman and was prepared to do anything to achieve greatness. She talked of killing King Duncan and spurred on Macbeth, who was reluctant to commit murder. She told him how the murder of the king was absolutely necessary to making the prophecy come true.

The king quite often used to visit his thanes and was coming to Macbeth's house. His two sons, Malcolm and Donalbain, and numerous thanes and attendants were all coming with him to honour Macbeth for his triumphal success in the war.

Macbeth's castle was pleasantly situated and the air about it was fresh and clean. Swallows had built their nests under all the jutting ledges of the building and these birds only live in places where the air is good. The king was pleased with the place and with the attentions and respect of his hostess, Lady Macbeth. She had the art of hiding treacherous purposes with smiles and could look like an innocent flower, while all the time, she was the snake under it.

The king was tired after his journey and went to bed early. Two servants slept beside him as was the custom. He had been unusually pleased with his reception and given presents to his chief officers. He had also sent a rich diamond to Lady Macbeth and described her as his most kind hostess.

It was the middle of night when nature seems dead and wicked dreams haunt sleeping men's minds and no one except the wolf and the murderer is about. This was the time when Lady Macbeth awoke to plot the murder of the king. She would not have undertaken such an unwomanly deed, but that she was afraid her husband was too kind to do it. She knew he was ambitious, but he still knew the difference between right and wrong and was not yet ready to be really wicked in the way that greedy ambition demands. She had won him over to the idea of murder, but she wasn't sure he would stick to his plan. She was afraid that the gentle feelings would come between him and his decision to kill the king and he wouldn't do it. She took the dagger up to the king's bedroom. She had already made sure the servants had drunk so much wine that they slept in a stupor, taking no care of their charge. There lay Duncan in a sound sleep after the efforts of his journey. She looked at him carefully, there was something in his face which reminded her of her own father. She didn't feel brave enough to kill him there and then.

She returned to discuss it with her husband. He was feeling a bit unsure. He thought that there were strong reasons against the murder. In the first place, he was not only a subject, but a near relative of the king. He was the king's host whose duty, by the law of hospitality, it was to lock out murderers, not to stab the king himself. Then he considered how just and merciful a king Duncan had been; he had been fair to the ordinary people and very kind to his thanes, particularly to Macbeth himself. Kings like Duncan are in the special care of Heaven and their subjects are doubly bound to avenge their deaths. Besides, because he was a favourite of the king, Macbeth had a good reputation among all sorts of men. All these honours would be stained by the news of so foul a murder!

Lady Macbeth found her husband in this troubled state, inclining to the better way and deciding to go no further. She was a woman who was not easily shaken from her purpose, and began to pour words in his ears which infused a portion of her own strong willpower into his mind. She gave him reason upon reason why he should not shrink from what he had undertaken. How easy it would be, how soon it would be over and how the action of one short night would give all their nights and days to come royalty! Then she mocked him and accused him of being a coward. She said that she had a child and knew how tender her feelings were when she cuddled her baby, but she would, while it was smiling up at her, have pulled it from her arms and dashed its brains out, if she had promised to do so as he had promised to murder Duncan. Then she added how easy it was to make the drunken sleepy servants look guilty. She stirred up his feelings and courage so much that he once more felt brave enough to do the horrid deed.

So taking the dagger in his hand, he softly crept into the dark to the bedroom where Duncan lay asleep and, as he went, he thought he saw another dagger in the air, with the handle towards him. On the blade and at the point of it were drops of blood, but when he tried to grasp it, it was nothing but air.

Putting his fear aside, he went into the king's room and stabbed him. Just as he had done the murder, one of the servants laughed in his sleep and the orther cried 'Murder!' This woke them both up, but they said a short prayer. One of them said, 'God bless us!' and the other answered 'Amen!' and they went back to sleep again. Macbeth, who stood listening to them, tried to say 'Amen', when the servant said, 'God bless us!' but, though he had most need of blessing, the word stuck in his throat and he was unable to say it.

He thought he heard a voice which cried, 'Sleep no more! Macbeth murders sleep, the innocent sleep that nourishes life.' It carried on, 'Sleep no more!' to all the house. 'Glamis has murdered sleep, so Cawdor shall sleep no more. Macbeth shall sleep no more.'

With these horrible imaginings Macbeth returned to his wife. She had begun to think he had failed. He arrived in so distracted a state that she complained of how weak he was. She sent him to wash the blood off his hands, while she took his dagger to wipe on the servants to make them seem guilty.

Morning came and with it, the discovery of the murder. Macbeth and Lady Macbeth made a great show of sadness. The proof against the servants — they were found smeared with blood and with the dagger still in the room — was strong, yet suspicion still fell upon Macbeth. After all, he had more to gain from such a deed than poor silly servants. Duncan's two sons ran away. Malcolm, the elder, went to England, while the younger, Donalbain, made his escape to Ireland.

The king's sons, who should have succeeded him, left the throne empty. Macbeth as next heir, was crowned king and so the prediction of the witches became true.

Although they now ruled Scotland, Macbeth and his queen could not forget the witches' prophecy that, although Macbeth should be king, it wasn't his children, but the children of Banquo, who were going to be kings after him. The thought of this and that they had done such a terrible crime only to place Banquo's family on the throne, so rankled them that they decided to kill both Banquo and his son. This would prevent the witches' prophecy coming true for Banquo as it had for Macbeth. So they invited all the chief thanes to a banquet. They made a special point of inviting Banquo and his son

Fleance. On the way to Macbeth's castle Banquo was set upon by murderers employed by Macbeth. Banquo was stabbed to death but in the scuffle Fleance escaped. Fleance became the grandfather of kings who occupied the Scottish throne, ending with James VI of Scotland and I of England, under whom the two crowns of England and Scotland were united.

At the banquet, the queen, whose manners were charming and royal, played the hostess with grace and attention to all her guests. Macbeth chatted freely with the thanes, saying that all the finest people in the country were under his roof, except his good friend Banquo. He said that he hoped he should only have to tell Banquo off for being late rather than worry because he'd had an accident. At these words, the ghost of Banquo entered the room and sat down on Macbeth's chair. Although Macbeth was a brave man, who could have faced the devil without trembling, his cheeks turned white with fear at this horrible sight and he stood terrified with his eyes fixed upon the ghost.

His queen and all the thanes, who saw nothing but an empty chair, took it for a fit of distraction. Lady Macbeth told him off, whispering that it was only the same imagining that had made him see the dagger in the air when he was about to kill Duncan. Macbeth continued to see the ghost and paid no attention to anything anyone said. He spoke to the ghost in distracted words, but their meaning seemed clear enough to Lady Macbeth that she was worried that the dreadful secret would be revealed. Quickly she sent the guests home, excusing Macbeth's behaviour as an illness he was often troubled with.

Macbeth was full of dreadful imaginings and he and his queen had their sleep disturbed by terrible dreams. More than the murder of Banquo, they were troubled by the escape of Fleance, whom they now realized would be the father of a line of kings instead of their own children. These miserable thoughts gave them no peace and Macbeth decided to look for the witches once more and learn the worst.

He found them in a cave on the heath. They knew he was coming and were busy preparing their dreadful charms to conjure up devilish spirits to tell the future. Their horrid ingredients were toads, bats, snakes, a newt's eye, a dog's tongue, a lizard's leg, an owl's wing, a dragon's scale, a wolf's tooth, the stomach of the ravenous shark, the mummy of a witch, the root of poisonous hemlock dug up in the dark, the gallbladder of a goat, the liver of a Jew, pieces of a yew-tree rooted in a grave and the finger of a dead child. All these were set to boil in a great cauldron, which, as fast as it grew too hot, was cooled with a baboon's blood. Then they poured in the blood of a sow that had eaten her piglets and they threw into the flame the grease from a murderer's gibbet. With these spells they forced the devilish spirits to answer their questions.

The witches asked Macbeth whether he wanted his questions answered by them or by their masters, the spirits. He, not at all frightened by the dreadful ritual, boldly answered, 'Where are they? Let me see them.' They called the spirits. The first rose up and looked like a head wearing a helmet. He called Macbeth by name and told him be careful of the Thane of Fife. Macbeth thanked him, for he had always been jealous of Macduff, the Thane of Fife.

The second spirit looked like a bloodstained child. He called Macbeth by name and told him not to fear the power of man, for no one born by a woman could hurt him. He advised Macbeth to be bloody, bold and resolute.

'Then Macduff might just as well live!' cried the king. 'Why should I fear him? But I will make certainty twice as sure. I shall not let him live so that I may tell pale-hearted Fear that it lies and can sleep in spite of the thunder.'

A third spirit in the form of a crowned child, with a tree in his hand arose. He called

Macbeth by name and comforted him against plots saying that he should never be beaten until Birnam Wood should come to Dunsinane Hill.

'This is excellent!' cried Macbeth. 'Who can dig up the entire forest and move it? I see I shall live the usual length of a man's life and not be cut off by a violent death. But my heart yearns to know one thing. Tell me, if you can, if Banquo's children and grandchildren shall ever reign in this kingdom?'

The cauldron sank into the ground and music could be heard. Eight shadows, like kings, passed by Macbeth, followed by Banquo. The eighth king carried a mirror which showed the figures of many more kings and Banquo, covered with blood, smiled at Macbeth and pointed to them. Macbeth knew that these were Banquo's children and their children and their children who would reign after him in Scotland. The witches, with soft music and dancing, vanished.

The first thing Macbeth heard when he left the witches' cave, was that Macduff, Thane of Fife, had gone to England. He intended to join the army that Malcolm, the dead king's eldest son, was forming to lead against Macbeth. Macbeth, stung with rage, sent murderers to Macduff's castle. They killed his wife and children and every member of the family. All these actions made the Scottish thanes hate and loathe Macbeth.

Many went to join Malcolm and Macduff, who were now approaching with the powerful army that they had raised in England. The rest secretly wished them success but they were so afraid of Macbeth they could not join in the coming battle. Everybody hated the tyrant. Nobody loved or respected him; everyone suspected him. He began to envy the murdered Duncan, who slept soundly in his grave. Treason had done its worst to Duncan and he could no longer be hurt or disturbed by swords, poison, trouble in Scotland or foreign enemies.

Meanwhile, the queen, who had been the sole partner in his wickedness and like Macbeth himself had been haunted by terrible nightmares, died. Perhaps she killed herself unable to bear the guilt and hatred. So Macbeth was left alone, without a soul to love or care for him, or a friend to whom he could tell his wicked plans.

He stopped wanting to live and wished for death, but the approach of Malcolm's army roused what remained of his courage. He decided to die, as he expressed it, with armour on his back. In addition the promises of the witches had filled him with confidence. He remembered the saying of the spirits that nobody born of woman could hurt him and that he would never be beaten till Birnam Wood came to Dunsinane. He thought this could never happen. He shut himself up in his strong castle and waited for Malcolm and his army.

Almost immediately a messenger came to him. He was pale and shaking with fear, almost unable to say what he had seen. He said that, as he stood on look-out-duty on the hill, he looked towards Birnam and it seemed that the woods began to move!

'Liar!' screamed Macbeth. 'If you are lying, I shall hang you up alive on the tree till you die of hunger. If you are speaking the truth, then I don't care if you do the same thing to me.' Macbeth's determination was beginning to weaken and he started to doubt the words of the spirits. He had no reason to be afraid till Birnam Wood came to Dunsinane — and now the wood was moving. 'However,' he said, 'if what he says is true, let us put on our armour and go out. There is no point running away and no point staying here. I am growing tired and wish my life at an end.' With these desperate words he burst out of the castle.

The strange event which had given the messenger the idea that the wood was moving is easily solved. When Malcolm's army marched through Birnam Wood, he had instructed each of his soldiers to cut down a branch and carry it in front of him to disguise the true numbers of soldiers. The soldiers with branches in front of them had, at a distance, looked like a wood on the move. So the words of the spirit came true, but in quite a different way from how Macbeth had understood them.

Now a fierce battle took place. Macbeth, though feebly supported by those who called themselves his friends, fought furiously and bravely, cutting to pieces anyone who opposed him. Finally, he came to where Macduff was fighting. Macbeth remembered the warning spirit who had advised him to be careful of Macduff more than any other man. He would have turned away, but Macduff, who had been looking for him through the whole battle, rushed at him and a fierce fight followed. Macduff complained bitterly about the murder of his wife and children. Macbeth, who was already guilty enough of that family's deaths, would still have avoided the fight, but Macduff still urged him to it, calling him tyrant, murderer, hell-hound, and villain.

Then Macbeth remembered the words of the spirit, how no one born of woman could hurt him. Smiling confidently, he said to Macduff, 'You are wasting your energy, Macduff. You can just as easily wound the air with your sword as hurt me. I have a charmed life, which cannot be taken by anyone born of woman.'

'Despair of your charm,' said Macduff. 'That lying spirit should have told you that I was never born of woman in the usual way but by surgery when doctors brought me into the world before I was expected.'

'Curse the tongue that tells me this!' said the trembling Macbeth, who felt his last hold of confidence give way, 'and never let anyone ever believe again the lying riddles of witches and cheating spirits, who deceive us in words which have double meaning. While they keep their promise literally, they disappoint our hopes with a different meaning. I will not fight you.'

'Then live!' said Macduff scornfully. 'We will put you on show, as men show monsters. We will put up a sign on which shall be written, "Here men may see the tyrant!"'

'Never!' said Macbeth, whose courage returned with despair. 'I will not stay alive to kiss the ground before young Malcolm's feet and to be mocked with the curses of the mob. Though Birnam Wood has come to Dunsinane, and you, who were never born of woman, are against me, I will still try.' With these frantic words, he hustled against Macduff. After a terrible fight, Macduff finally beat him. He cut off the dead Macbeth's head and made a present of it to the young and lawful king, Malcolm. The new king ascended the throne of Duncan amid the cheers of the thanes and the people.

All's Well that Ends Well

Bertram had just become Count of Rousillon as his father had recently died. The King of France had been very fond of Bertram's father and when he heard of his death, he sent for Bertram to come to his royal court in Paris immediately.

Bertram was living with his widowed mother, when Lafeu, an old lord of the French court, came to take him to the king. An invitation to the court was more like an order in those days and nobody, even princes, dukes and counts, dared to refuse. The old countess was very sad to part with her much-loved son, but she dared not delay him a single day and immediately gave orders for his departure. Lafeu tried to comfort the countess both for the death of her husband and her son's sudden absence. He told her that the king was so kind, she would find him thoughtful as her husband and that he would be like a second father to her son. He meant that the good king would become Bertram's friend. Lafeu told the countess that the king had become ill and his doctors said that the illness was incurable. The countess was sorry to hear this and she said she wished Gerard de Narbon was still alive. He was the father of Helena, a young woman who was living with her. She had no doubt that he could have cured the king. She told Lafeu about Helena, saying that she was the only daughter of the famous physician Gerard de Narbon. He had asked her to look after Helena when he was dying, and since his death Helena had lived in her house. Then the countess praised Helena's goodness, gentleness and kindness, saying that she had inherited these qualities from her father. While the countess was speaking, Helena was sitting, crying quietly. This made the countess tell her off very gently for too much sadness over her father's death.

Bertram now said goodbye to his mother. She parted with her dear son with tears

and blessings, and asked Lafeu to take care of him, saying, 'My lord, advise him, for he is not used to court life.'

Bertram's last words were spoken to Helena, but they were merely of politeness, wishing her happiness. He finished his short goodbye to her by saying, 'Comfort my mother and make much of her.'

Helena had loved Bertram for a long time and when she was crying so quietly, her tears were not for her father. Helena had loved her father, but the immediate prospect of Bertram's departure for the court upset her so much that she had even forgotten what her father looked like. She could think only of Bertram.

Although Helena had loved Bertram for a long time, she never forgot that he was the Count of Rousillon and a member of the most ancient family in France. She was an ordinary girl — there were no dukes or counts in her family. So she looked up to the high-born Bertram as to her dear lord, and dared not wish more than to live as his servant. She used to think to herself, 'It is just the same as if I loved a particular bright star and thought to marry it; Bertram is so far above me.'

Bertram's absence filled her eyes with tears and her heart with sadness. Although she loved him without hope, it was still a comfort to her to see him. Helena would sit and look at his dark eyes, his arched brows and the curls of his fine hair till she seemed to draw his portrait on her heart.

When Gerard de Narbon died, he had no money to leave her, only some prescriptions for rare but tried and tested medicines. He had studied hard and been a doctor for a long time, so he had collected powerful and effective cures. Among them was a prescription for a medicine to treat the disease that Lafeu had said the king was suffering from. When Helena heard of the king's illness, she formed an ambitious project in her mind. She decided to go to Paris and cure the king. However, although she was the owner of this perfect prescription, it was unlikely that the king and his doctors would take any notice of her, especially as they thought his disease was incurable. Helena's certainty of success, if she were allowed to try her cure, seemed more than her father's skill warranted, even though he was the most famous doctor of his time. She believed that the medicine was the key to her hopes and her future.

Bertram had not been gone long, when the countess's steward told her that he had overheard Helena talking to herself. Her words suggested that she was in love with Bertram and thought of following him to Paris. The countess thanked her steward and asked him to tell Helena that she wished to talk to her. What she had just heard of Helena reminded her of days long past, when her love for Bertram's father first began. She

said to herself, 'I felt just like that when I was young. Love can be very painful.' While the countess was thinking about her first young feelings of love, Helena came in. The countess said to her, 'Helena, you know I am like a mother to you.'

Helena replied, 'You are my respected mistress.'

'You are a daughter to me,' said the countess again. 'I say I am your mother. Why do you look startled and pale at my words?'

Looking worried and feeling confused, and afraid that the countess suspected her love, Helena replied, 'Pardon me, madam, you are not my mother. The Count of Rousillon cannot be my brother, nor can I be your daughter.'

'Yet, Helena,' the countess said, 'you might be my daughter-in-law. The words *mother* and *daughter* so disturb you. Helena, do you love my son?'

'Good madam, pardon me,' said Helena in fright.

Again the countess repeated her question, 'Do you love my son?'

'Don't you love him, madam?' asked Helena.

The countess replied, 'Don't side-step the question, Helena. Come, come, tell me all about your feelings, for your love has become obvious.'

Helena, on her knees, now admitting her love and with shame and terror implored the pardon of her mistress. She explained that she fully understood that he was a count and she was just an ordinary girl and said that Bertram did not know she loved him. The countess then asked Helena if she intended to go to Paris. Helena admitted the plan she had formed in her mind when she heard Lafeu speak of the king's illness.

'Was it really your reason for wanting to go to Paris,' said the countess, 'was it? Speak truly.'

Helena answered honestly, 'The count, your son, made me think of this. Otherwise, Paris, the medicine and the king would not have crossed my mind.'

The countess heard all this without saying a word either of approval or blame, but she questioned Helena closely about the probability of the medicine being helpful to the king. She found that it was the most highly-prized of Gerard de Narbon's possessions and that he had given it to his daughter on his death-bed. She remembered the solemn promise she had made to Helena's father and realized that the girl's future and the life of the king himself depended on her carrying out this project. She gave Helena permission to go to Paris and generously provided her with money and suitable attendants. So Helena set out for Paris with the blessing of the countess and her kindest wishes for her success.

Helena arrived at Paris and, with the help of her friend the old Lord Lafeu, she was taken to see the king. She had still many difficulties ahead, for the king was not easily persuaded to try the medicine offered to him by this pretty young doctor. She told him she was Gerard de Narbon's daughter and the king remembered the famous doctor. She offered the special medicine as the greatest treasure of all her father's long experience and skill and she bravely stated that she was prepared to die if it failed to restore the king to perfect health within two days. The king at last agreed to try it, but if he did not recover in two days' time, Helena was to lose her life. If she succeeded, however, he promised to give her the choice of any man throughout all France apart from the princes, as a husband. This was the payment Helena demanded if she cured the king of his disease.

Helena was not wrong about her father's medicine. Before two days were at an end, the king was restored to perfect health. He called all the young noblemen of his court together so that Helena could choose a husband. Helena was not slow to make her choice, for among these young men she saw the Count Rousillon. Turning to Bertram, she said, 'This is the man. I dare not say I take you, but I give myself to you.'

'Why, then,' said the king, 'young Bertram, take her, she is your wife.'

Bertram wasted no time in explaining how much he disliked this idea. He pointed out that Helena was a poor doctor's daughter, now living on his mother's generosity. Helena heard him speak these words of rejection and scorn. She said to the king, 'I'm just glad you are well, my lord. Let the rest go.' The king, however, would not allow his royal command to be ignored, for arranging the marriages of his nobles was one of his

many royal privileges. That same day Bertram was married to Helena. It was a forced and uneasy marriage for Bertram did not offer much hope to poor Helena — the king could not force her new husband to love her.

No sooner were they married than Bertram asked Helena to apply to the king for permission for him to leave the court. When she brought him the king's permission, Bertram told her that, as he had not been prepared for this sudden marriage, it had unsettled him and so she should not be surprised by his action. If Helena was not surprised, she was certainly sad when she found that he planned to leave her. He ordered her to go home to his mother. When Helena heard this unkind command, she replied, 'I can say nothing to this but that I am your most obedient servant.' These humble words did not move Bertram to pity his gentle wife, however, and he parted from her without even the common politeness of a kind goodbye.

Helena returned to the countess. She had succeeded with her plans; she had saved the king's life and she had married the man she loved but she returned a very sad lady to her noble mother-in-law. As soon as she entered the house, she received a letter from Bertram which almost broke her heart.

The good old countess welcomed her warmly, as if she had been her son's own choice and a noble lady. She comforted her for Bertram's unkind neglect in sending his wife home alone on her wedding day, but this kindness failed to cheer up Helena. She said, 'Madam, my lord is gone for ever!' She then read these words out of Bertram's letter: *When you can get the ring from my finger, which never shall come off, then call me husband, but when I write then I really mean never.* 'This is dreadful!' said Helena.

The countess begged her to have patience and said now Bertram was gone, she should be her child. She told Helena that she deserved a better husband with twenty such rude boys as Bertram as servants. All this kindness and friendliness still could not soothe poor Helena's feelings. She still kept her eyes fixed on the letter, and cried out in misery, 'Till I have no wife, I have nothing in France.'

The countess asked her if those words were written in the letter?

'Yes, madam,' was all poor Helena could answer.

The next morning Helena was missing. She had left a letter to be given to the countess after she was gone to explain her sudden absence. In this letter Helena informed her that she was so upset at having driven Bertram from his own country and his own home that she had gone on a pilgrimage to the shrine of St Jacques le Grand. She asked the countess to tell Bertram that the wife he hated so much had left his house for ever.

When Bertram left Paris, he went to Florence, where he became an officer in the

Duke of Florence's army. After a successful war, in which he had shown great bravery, Bertram received letters from his mother. These told him that Helena would not be a nuisance to him any longer. He was just getting ready to return home, when Helena herself, dressed in the plain clothes of a pilgrim, arrived in Florence.

Pilgrims used to pass through Florence on their way to St Jacques le Grand. When Helena arrived there, she learned that a friendly widow who lived there offered a place for the female pilgrims to stay. Helena went to see this good lady and the widow gave her a kind welcome. She invited her to see the sights of that famous city and told her that if she would like to see the duke's army, she would take Helena where she might have a good view of it. 'And you will see a countryman of yours,' said the widow, 'his name is Count Rousillon, who has done well in the duke's wars.'

Helena did not need a second invitation when she found Bertram was to be part of the show. She went with her hostess and it was a pleasure to look at her dear husband's face again.

'Isn't he a handsome man?' said the widow.

'I like him,' replied Helena, with great truth.

All the time they were talking, the talkative widow's conversation was full of Bertram. She told Helena the story of Bertram's marriage and how he had deserted his poor wife and joined the duke's army to avoid living with her. Helena listened patiently

to her own story. When the widow had finished this story, she started another tale. Every word she spoke sank deep into Helena's mind for the story she now told was of Bertram's love for her own daughter.

Although Bertram did not like the marriage forced on him by the king, it seems he was not unable to fall in love. Since he had been with the army in Florence, he had fallen in love with Diana, a pretty young girl and the daughter of Helena's hostess. Every night, with music and songs written about Diana's beauty, he would stand under her window and ask his love to love him. He would plead with her to let him visit her secretly after the family had gone to bed but Diana would not agree. Knowing him to be married, she paid no attention for she had been brought up by a wise mother.

The good lady told all this to Helena, praising the good behaviour of her sensible daughter, which, she said, was entirely a result of the excellent education and good advice she had given her. She added that Bertram had been particularly demanding of Diana, pleading with her to let him visit her that night because he was going to leave Florence early the next morning.

Although it upset Helena to hear of Bertram's love for the widow's daughter, her clever brain developed a plan from this story. She was not at all discouraged by the failure of her first plan. She told the widow that she was Helena, Bertram's deserted wife, and she asked her and her daughter to agree to Bertram's visit. However, she would pretend to be Diana. Then she told her main reason for wanting to have this secret meeting with her husband was to get a ring from him, for he had said that if ever she had the ring, he would treat her as his wife.

The widow and her daughter promised to help her partly because they felt sorry for her and partly because she promised them a reward. To show that she would keep her word, Helena gave them a purse of money. During that day, Helena arranged for Bertram to be told that she had died, hoping that when he thought himself free to make a second choice by the news of her death, he would ask her to marry him while she was disguised as Diana. She was sure that if she could obtain the ring and a promise of marriage she could make some good come of it.

In the evening, after it was dark, Bertram was allowed into Diana's room and Helena was waiting for him. The charming things and loving words he spoke to Helena were precious to her, although she knew they were really meant for Diana. Bertram was so delighted with her that he made a solemn promise to marry her and to love her for ever. She hoped that this would come true when he discovered that it was his own wife, the hated Helena, whose conversation had so delighted him.

Bertram had never realized how sensitive Helena was, otherwise he probably would not have ignored her. Because he used to see her every day, he had entirely overlooked her beauty. A face we are used to seeing constantly soon stops having any effect. It was impossible for him to judge her mind because she felt he was so important and loved him so much that she was always silent in his presence. Now that her future and a happy ending to all her plans depended upon her making a favourable impression on Bertram that night, she did her best to please him. Her lively conversation and sweetness so charmed Bertram that he promised that he would marry her. Helena asked him for the ring from his finger as a sign of his love and he gave it to her. In return for his ring, which was of such importance to her, she gave him the ring that the king had given her. She sent Bertram away before dawn and he immediately set out on his journey towards his mother's house.

Helena persuaded the widow and Diana to come with her to Paris, because she needed more help from them to complete her plan. When they arrived, they found the king was visiting the Countess of Rousillon, so Helena followed the king as quickly as possible.

The king was still in perfect health. He was so grateful to Helena for his recovery that the moment he saw the Countess of Rousillon, he began to talk about her, calling her a precious jewel lost by the foolishness of her son. However, seeing that the subject upset the countess, who was truly sad over the death of Helena, he said, 'My good lady, I have forgiven and forgotten all.'

The good-natured old Lafeu, who could not bear that his favourite Helena should be so easily forgotten, said, 'This I must say: the young count insulted the king, his mother and his wife but the person he wronged most of all was himself for he has lost a wife whose beauty astonished all eyes, whose words took all ears captive, whose goodness made all hearts wish to serve her.'

The king said, 'Praising what is lost makes the memory dear. Well, call him here,' meaning Bertram. He now presented himself to the king and said how sorry he was for being so nasty to Helena. The king, for his dead father's and his admirable mother's sake, pardoned him and restored him once more to his favour. However, the king suddenly noticed that Bertram was wearing the very ring which he had given to Helena. He remembered that Helena had promised that she would never part with that ring unless she sent it to the king himself because something terrible had happened to her. When the king asked Bertram how he came by the ring, he told an improbable story about a lady throwing it to him out of a window. He said that he had never seen Helena since their wedding. The king knowing Bertram's dislike of his wife, was afraid that he had killed her and he ordered his guards to seize Bertram, saying, 'I am very worried for I fear that Helena has been murdered.'

At this moment Diana and her mother came in to ask a favour of the king. They wanted him to use his royal power to make Bertram marry Diana as he had promised. Bertram, fearing the king's anger, said that he had made no such promise and then Diana produced the ring which Helena had given her, to prove the truth of her words and she said that she had given Bertram the ring he was wearing at the time he promised to marry her. On hearing this, the king ordered the guards to seize her too. Her explanation was so different from Bertram's that the king was sure he was right about Helena's murder and he said that if they did not tell how they came by this ring of Helena's, they should both be put to death. Diana asked for her mother to be allowed to fetch the jeweller who sold her the ring. The king said she might and the widow went out. She soon returned, leading Helena herself.

The good countess had seen her son's danger and had even dreaded that the suspicion of his having murdered his wife might possibly be true. When she discovered that her dear Helena, whom she loved like a mother, was still living, she was so delighted she could hardly bear it. The king was so happy he could hardly believe his eyes and asked, 'Is this really the wife of Bertram that I see?'

Helena, still feeling that she was not a proper wife, replied, 'No, my lord, it is but the shadow of a wife you see, the name and not the person.'

Bertram cried out, 'Both, both! O, I'm sorry!'

Helena said, 'When I pretended to be this girl, I found you were very kind. Look, here is your letter!' She read out loud the words which had once made her so sad: *When*

you can get this ring from my finger. 'I have — it was to me you gave the ring. Will you be my real husband, now that you are doubly won?'

Bertram replied, 'If you can prove that you were the lady I talked to that night, I will love you for ever dearly.'

This was easy, for the widow and Diana had come with Helena purposely to prove this fact. The king was so delighted with Diana for the friendly help she had given Helena, whom he so valued for the service she had done him, that he promised her a noble husband. Helena's story suggested to him that it was a suitable reward for kings to give beautiful ladies when they perform special services.

So Helena at last found that her father's legacy had indeed brought her good luck. She was now the beloved wife of her dear Bertram, the daughter-in-law of her noble mistress and herself the Countess of Rousillon.

The Taming of the Shrew

Katharine was the elder daughter of Baptista, a rich gentleman of Padua in Italy. She had such a fierce tongue and fiery temper that she was known in Padua as Katharine the Shrew. It seemed very unlikely, indeed impossible, that anyone would ever want to marry her. So Baptista was often criticized for refusing to agree to many excellent offers made to her gentle sister Bianca, with the excuse that Katharine must be married first.

One day a man called Petruchio came from Verona to Padua to look for a wife. He wasn't at all discouraged by the reports of Katharine's temper, and hearing she was rich and beautiful, decided that he would marry her and tame this famous dragon into a meek and manageable wife. Truly nobody was more suitable to set about this difficult task as Petruchio, who was as strong-minded as Katharine. He was a witty, happy and humorous man. He was also both wise and clever so that he knew how to pretend to be furious, when he was really so calm that he could have laughed at his own angry shouting. In reality his natural temper was careless and easy.

Petruchio set about marrying Katharine the Shrew. First of all he asked Baptista for permission to talk of love to his *gentle daughter* Katharine, as Petruchio called her. He said that having heard of her bashful modesty and mild behaviour, he had come from Verona to win her love. Her father, although he wanted her to get married, was forced to admit Katharine could hardly be described like this. Just how gentle she was became obvious, for her music teacher rushed into the room to complain that the gentle Katharine, his pupil, had broken his head with her lute when he said that she played something wrongly. When Petruchio heard this, he said, 'She is a brave girl. I love her more than ever and long to chat with her.' Hurrying the old man to say yes, Petruchio said, 'I am in a hurry, Signor Baptista, I cannot come here every day to talk of love. You knew my father. He is dead and has left me all his lands and goods. Then tell me, if I win your daughter's love, what dowry will you give with her?'

Baptista thought his manner was somewhat blunt for a lover, but being glad to get Katharine married, he answered that he would give her twenty thousand crowns for her dowry and half his lands at his death. So this odd match was quickly agreed and Baptista went to tell his shrewish daughter of her Petruchio. Then he sent her in to Petruchio to listen to him.

In the meantime Petruchio was deciding how to go about winning Katharine's love, and he said to himself, 'I will talk to her with liveliness when she comes. If she shouts at me, then I will tell her she sings as sweetly as a nightingale. If she frowns, I will say she looks as clear as roses newly washed with dew. If she will not speak a word, I will praise the beauty of her language and if she asks me to leave her, I will give thanks to her warmly as if she asked me to stay with her a week.'

Now, Katharine came in and Petruchio greeted her with, 'Good morning, Kate, for that is your name, I hear.'

Katharine, not liking this plain greeting, said scornfully 'People who talk to me call me Katharine.'

'You lie,' Petruchio replied. 'For you are called plain Kate and bonny Kate and sometimes Kate the Shrew, but, Kate, you are the prettiest Kate in the world and so, Kate, hearing your mildness praised in every town, I have come to ask you to be my wife.'

A strange conversation followed. She was so loud and angry that she showed him how fairly she gained the name of Shrew, while he still praised her sweet and polite words. At last, hearing her father coming, he said, 'Sweet Katharine, let us set this idle chat aside, for your father has agreed that you shall be my wife, your dowry is agreed on, and whether you want to or not, I will marry you.'

When Baptista came in, Petruchio told him his daughter had been kind to him and that she had promised to be married the next Sunday. Katharine denied this, saying she would rather see him hanged on Sunday. She scolded her father for wishing to marry her to such a madcap ruffian as Petruchio. Petruchio asked him to take no notice of her angry words, because, he said, they had agreed she should seem unwilling in front of him, but that when they were alone he had found her very fond and loving. He said to her, 'Give me your hand, Kate. I wil go to Venice to buy you fine clothes for our wedding day. Provide the feast, father, and invite the wedding guests. I will be sure to bring rings and rich clothes so that my Katharine will look splendid. Kiss me, Kate, for we will be married on Sunday.'

On Sunday, all the wedding guests arrived, but they had to wait a long time before Petruchio came. Katharine cried out of irritation to think that Petruchio had only been making fun of her. Eventually he appeared, but he brought none of the wedding finery he had promised Katharine, nor was he dressed like a bridegroom. He was wearing strange, untidy clothes, as if he meant to make a joke of the serious business he came for. His servant and even the horses they rode also looked peculiar.

Petruchio could not be persuaded to change his clothes. He said Katharine was to be married to *him* and not to his clothes. Finding it was pointless to argue with him, they went to church with Petruchio still behaving in the same mad way. When the priest asked Petruchio if Katharine should be his wife, he said so loudly that she should that the amazed priest dropped his book, and, as he bent down to pick it up, this strange bridegroom pushed him over. All the time they were being married, he stamped and swore so that Katharine trembled and shook with fear. After the ceremony was over, while they were still in church, he called for wine and drank a loud toast to the company. Then he flicked wine in the sexton's face, for no other reason than that the sexton's beard was thin and straggly. There never was such a mad wedding.

Baptista provided a wonderful banquet, but when they returned from church, Petruchio took hold of Katharine and announced that he was taking his wife home instantly. No protest from his father-in-law nor angry words from the furious Katharine could make him change his mind. He claimed a husband's right to do as he pleased with his wife and hurried Katharine off. He seemed so daring and determined that no one dared try to stop him.

Petruchio put his wife on a miserable skinny horse, which he had specially chosen for her and he and his servant mounted their horses. They travelled on muddy roads and even when the horse of Katharine's stumbled, he would storm and swear at the poor animal which could scarcely crawl under its load.

At last, after a weary journey, during which Katharine had heard nothing but the wild ravings of Petruchio at his servant and the horses, they arrived at his house. Petruchio welcomed her kindly to her new home, but he made up his mind that she should have neither sleep nor food that night. The table was spread and supper was soon served, but Petruchio, pretending to find fault with every dish, threw the meat on the floor and ordered the servants to remove it. He did this, he said, out of love for his Katharine because he did not want her to eat meat that was not well cooked. When Katharine, tired and supperless, went to bed, he found the same fault with that, throwing the pillows and bedclothes about the room. She was forced to sit down in a chair where, if she chanced to fall asleep, she was woken up by the loud voice of her husband storming at the servants for making his wife's bridal bed so badly.

The next day Petruchio carried on in the same way, still speaking kindly to Katharine but when she attempted to eat, he found fault with everything that was put in front of her and threw breakfast on the floor as he had done supper. Poor proud Katharine was forced to ask the servants to bring her a bite of food secretly, but they, having been instructed by Petruchio, replied that they dare not give her anything without telling him first.

'Ah!' she said, 'did he marry me to starve me? Beggars who come to my father's door have food given to them, but I, who have never had to ask for anything, am starved for lack of food and giddy for lack of sleep. What is even more irritating is that he does it under the name of perfect love, pretending that if I sleep or eat, I will die on the spot.' Here her thoughts were interrupted by Petruchio. Not intending her to starve completely, he had brought her a small portion of meat.

He said to her, 'How are you, my sweet Kate? Here, love, see how attentive I am. I have cooked your meat myself. I am sure this kindness deserves thanks. What, not a word? No, then you do not love the meat and all the effort I have made is pointless.' He then ordered the servant to take the dish away.

Extreme hunger had reduced Katharine's pride and made her say, though it angered her to do so, 'Please, leave it.'

However, this was not enough for Petruchio and he replied: 'The smallest kindness is repaid with thanks and you must thank me before you touch the meat.'

At this Katharine brought out a reluctant 'Thank you.'

Now he let her eat her little snack saying, 'Much good may it do your gentle heart, Kate. Eat up! And now, my honey love, we will return to your father's house and have a splendid party, with silk coats and caps and golden rings, with ruffs and scarfs and fans and two changes of fine clothes.' To convince her that he really intended to give her these lovely things, he called in a dressmaker and a hatter, who brought some new clothes he had ordered for her. Then before she had half satisfied her hunger he gave her plate to the servant to take away, saying, 'Have you finished?'

The hatter presented a cap, saying, 'Here is the cap you ordered.' At this Petruchio began to storm again, saying the cap was moulded in a bowl and that it was no bigger than a cockle or walnut-shell. He told the hatter to take it away and make a bigger one.

Katharine said, 'I will have this. All gentlewomen wear caps like this.'

'When you are gentle,' replied Petruchio, 'you shall have one, too. Not till then.'

The meat Katharine had eaten had revived her fallen spirits little, and she said, 'Sir, I trust I am allowed to speak and speak I will. I am not a child nor a baby. Better people than you have had to hear me say my mind and if you cannot, you had better block your ears.'

Petruchio would not listen to these angry words, for he had a better way of managing his wife than keeping up an argument with her. So he answered, 'What you say is true. It is a nasty cap and I love you for not liking it.'

'Love me or not,' Katharine said, 'I like the cap and I will have this one or nothing at all.'

'You say you wish to see the dress?' asked Petruchio, still pretending to misunderstand her. The dressmaker then came forward and showed her a beautiful dress he had made for her. Petruchio, who had no intention of letting her have either the cap or the dress, found fault with that. 'O, Heaven!' he said. 'What tatty stuff is here? Do you call this a sleeve? It looks like a tube. The dress is carved up and down like an apple tart.'

The dressmaker said, 'You asked me to make it fashionable.'

Katharine said she never saw a more fashionable dress. This was enough for Petruchio. He intended to pay these people for their goods and explain his strange treatment of them in private. With fierce words and furious gestures he drove the dressmaker and the hatter out of the room. Turning to Katharine, he said, 'Well, come, my Kate, we will go to your father's even in these plain clothes we are wearing now.'

Then he ordered his horses, saying that they should reach Baptista's house by dinner time for it was only seven o'clock. Now it was not early morning but the very middle of

the day when he said this. So, Katharine dared to answer although she spoke modestly, as she was overcome by his forceful manner. 'I dare tell you, sir, it is two o'clock and will be supper time before we get there.'

Petruchio intended her to be so completely subdued that she should agree with everything he said before he took her to her father's house. So, as if he were the lord of the sun itself and could command the hours, he said it should be what time he pleased to have it, before he set out. 'For,' he said, 'whatever I say or do, you still are crossing it. I will not go today and when I go, it shall be what time I say it is.' So Katharine was forced to practice her obedience for another day and Petruchio would not take her to see her father till he had made his proud Katharine so well behaved that she dared not remember there was even such a word as no. Even while they were on their way, she was in danger of being turned back again, only because she happened to hint it was the sun, when he stated that the moon shone brightly at midday.

'Now, by my mother's son,' he said, 'and that is me, it shall be the moon or stars or what I like, before I travel to your father's house.' He then looked as if he were going back again but Katharine, no longer Katharine the Shrew, but the obedient wife, said, 'Let us go forward, please, now that we have come so far. It shall be the sun or moon or what you please, and if you want to call it a candle, I promise I shall too.'

He decided to test her, so he said again, 'I say it is the moon.'

'I know it is the moon,' Katharine replied.

'You lie, it is the blessed sun,' said Petruchio.

'Then it is the blessed sun,' Katharine replied. 'But it is not the sun when you say it is not. What you will have it named, so it is, and so it shall be for ever for me.'

Now, he let her carry on with her journey, but to see if this gentle mood would last, he spoke to an old man they met on the road as if he had been a young woman. He said to him, 'Good morning, miss,' and asked Katharine if she had ever seen a prettier girl. He praised the old man's rosy cheeks and compared his eyes to two bright stars. Again he spoke to him, saying, 'Pretty girl, once more good day to you!' He said to his wife, 'Sweet Kate, give her a kiss for beauty's sake.'

Now, completely beaten Katharine quickly adopted her husband's opinion and spoke to the old man in the same way. She said, 'Young woman, you are pretty and fresh and sweet. Where are you going and where do you live? You are so pretty, your parents must be very happy.'

'What on earth are you talking about, Kate?' Petruchio said. 'I hope you haven't gone mad. This is a man, old and wrinkled, faded and withered, and not a girl, as you say he is.'

At this, Katharine said, 'Pardon me, old gentleman. The sun has dazzled my eyes so that everything I see seems young. Now I see that you are a gentleman. I hope you will excuse me for my silly mistake.'

'Do, good sir,' Petruchio said, 'and tell us which way you are travelling. We shall be glad of your company if you are going our way.'

The old man replied, 'Our strange meeting has amazed me. My name is Vincentio and I am going to visit my son who lives in Padua.'

Petruchio realized that the old man was the father of Lucentio, the young man who was about to marry Baptista's younger daughter, Bianca. He made Vincentio very happy by telling him of the splendid marriage his son was about to make and they all

travelled on pleasantly together till they came to Baptista's house. A lot of people had arrived there to celebrate Bianca's wedding for Baptista had agreed willingly to the marriage of Bianca once he had got Katharine off his hands.

Baptista welcomed them to the wedding party and told them that there was another bride and groom also celebrating. Lucentio, Bianca's husband, and Hortensio, the other bridegroom, could not stop making jokes about the shrewish character of Petruchio's wife. They both seemed highly pleased with the mild tempers of the wives they had chosen and laughed at Petruchio for his unlucky choice. Petruchio took little notice of their jokes till the ladies went off on their own after dinner. Then he noticed Baptista joined in the laughter against him. When Petruchio said that his wife would prove more obedient than theirs, Katharine's father said, 'Now, Petruchio, I am afraid you have got the truest shrew of all.'

'Well,' said Petruchio, 'I say no. To prove that I am telling the truth, let us each send for his wife and whichever wife is most obedient and comes when she is sent for shall win the bet.'

The other two husbands willingly agreed to this, for they were quite sure that their gentle wives would prove more obedient than the headstrong Katharine. They suggested a bet of twenty crowns, but Petruchio merrily said, he would bet as much as that on his hawk or hound. He was willing to bet twenty times as much upon his wife. Lucentio and Hortensio raised the bet to a hundred crowns and Lucentio was the first to send a servant to ask Bianca to come to him.

The servant returned and said, 'Sir, madam sends you a message that she is busy and cannot come.'

'Well!' Petruchio said. 'She says she is busy and cannot come. Is that an answer for a wife?'

Then they laughed at him and said it would be surprising if Katharine did not send a worse answer.

Now it was Hortensio's turn to send for his wife and he said to his servant, 'Go and ask my wife urgently to come to me.'

'Oh! ask her urgently!' Petruchio said. 'Then she must come.'

'I am afraid, sir,' said Hortensio, 'your wife will not be persuaded at all.' Soon, however, this husband looked a little blank, when the servant returned without his mistress. He said to him, 'Where is my wife?'

'Sir,' said the servant, 'Madam says you are having a good joke of some sort and she will not come. She asks you to come to her.'

'Worse and worse!' said Petruchio. Then he sent his servant, saying, 'Go to your mistress and tell her I order her to come to me.'

The men had scarcely time to imagine how she would respond to this when Baptista, in total amazement, exclaimed, 'Now, by heaven, here comes Katharine!'

She entered, saying meekly to Petruchio, 'What do you want me to do?'

'Where is your sister and Hortensio's wife?' he asked.

Katharine replied, 'They are sitting chatting by the parlour fire.'

'Go and bring them here!' Petruchio said. Without replying Katharine hurried off to carry out her husband's command.

'This is a miracle,' said Lucentio.

'It certainly is,' Hortensio said. 'I wonder what it means.'

'It means peace,' Petruchio said, 'and love and a quiet life, and proper rules. In short, everything that is sweet and happy.'

Katharine's father, overjoyed to see this change in his daughter, said, 'Good luck to you Petruchio! You have won the bet and I will add another twenty thousand crowns to her wedding present just as if she were another daughter, for she is changed as if she had never been.'

'No,' said Petruchio, 'I will win the bet still further and show more signs of her new goodness and obedience.' Katharine came in with the other two girls. He continued, 'See, there she comes and brings your disobedient wives as prisoners through her gentle persuasion. Katharine, that cap of yours does not suit you. Take it off and throw it on the floor.'

Katharine instantly took off her cap and threw it down.

'Lord!' said Hortensio's wife, 'I hope I never end up so silly!'

Bianca, too, said, 'What foolish duty do you call this?'

'At this,' Bianca's husband said her, 'I wish your duty were as foolish too. The wisdom of your duty, Bianca, has cost me a hundred crowns since dinner time.'

'The more fool you,' said Bianca, 'for betting on my duty.'

'Katharine,' said Petruchio, 'I ask you to tell these headstrong women what duty they should show their husbands.'

To the wonder of everyone there, the once shrewish Katharine spoke clearly in praise of the wife-like duty of obedience. Katharine once more became famous in Padua, not as before, as Katharine the Shrew, but as Katharine the most obedient and gentle wife in the city.

The Comedy of Errors

The states of Syracuse and Ephesus were not friendly and so there was a cruel law made at Ephesus that said that if any merchant of Syracuse was seen in the city of Ephesus, he was to be put to death unless he could pay a thousand marks. Ægeon, an old merchant of Syracuse, was caught in the streets of Ephesus and brought to the duke, either to pay this heavy fine or to receive sentence of death. Ægeon had no money to pay the fine. The duke, before he pronounced the sentence of death upon the old man, wished him to tell the story of his life and explain why he had dared to come to the city of Ephesus and put himself in such danger.

Ægeon said that he was not afraid to die because he was so sad that he was tired of his life, but that he could not have been asked to do anything more upsetting than having to tell the story of his unfortunate life. He then began.

'I was born in Syracuse and became a merchant. I got married and lived very happily with my wife. One day I had to go to Epidamnum on business and stayed there six months. Then, finding that I had to stay some time longer, I sent for my wife. As soon as she arrived, she gave birth to two sons. What was very strange was that they were so exactly alike that it was impossible to tell one from the other. At the same time that my wife had twins, a poor woman in the inn where my wife was staying also gave birth to two sons and her twins were just as much alike each other as my two sons were. The parents of these children were very poor, so I adopted the two boys and brought them up to become servants to my sons.

'My sons were very fine children and my wife was extremely proud of them. She longed to return home and I unwillingly agreed. We had not sailed more than a short distance from Epidamnum when a dreadful storm arose. It was so violent that the sailors, seeing no chance of saving the ship, crowded into the life-boat to save their own lives, leaving us alone on board. We expected that the fury of the storm would wreck the ship at any moment.

'The non-stop crying of my wife and the terrible wailing of the babies who, not understanding what was wrong, cried because they saw their mother cry, filled me with terror for them although I did not myself fear death. All my thoughts were concentrated on saving them. I tied my younger son to the end of a small spare mast; at the other end I fastened the younger of the twin servant boys. I explained to my wife how to secure the other children in the same way to another mast. She took charge of the two elder children and I took charge of the two younger ones. We tied ourselves separately to these masts with the children. If we hadn't done this we would have drowned for the ship split on a huge rock and was dashed to pieces. We clung to those thin masts and floated on the water. I was taking care of two children and was unable to assist my wife. She and the other two children were soon separated from me, but while they were still in sight, I saw them rescued by a fishing boat that I supposed came from Corinth. Seeing them safe, I had no other concerns except to struggle with the wild waves to save my dear son and the younger servant. At last we in our turn were rescued by a ship and the sailors, knowing me, gave us a kind welcome. We landed in safety at Syracuse but from that sad hour, I have never known what became of my wife and the elder child.

'When he was eighteen years old, my younger son began to be inquisitive about his mother and his brother and often asked me permission to take his servant, who had also lost his brother, and go in search of them. At last I unwillingly agreed, for though I anxiously wanted to hear news of my wife and elder son, in sending my younger one to find them, I risked losing him too. It is now seven years since my son left me. I have spent five years travelling through the world in search of him. I have been in farthest Greece and through Asia. Travelling homeward, I landed here in Ephesus because I was unwilling to leave any place without looking for him, but today must end the story of my life. I should think myself happy in my death, if I were certain my wife and sons were living.'

Here the ill-fated Ægeon ended the account of his bad luck. The duke pitied the unfortunate father who had brought this danger upon himself by his love for his lost son. He said that were it not against the laws, which he could not change, he would freely pardon him. However, instead of dooming him to instant death, as the strict letter of the law required, he would give him a day to try to beg or borrow the money to pay the fine.

This day of grace did not seem any great favour to Ægeon, for not knowing any man in Ephesus, there seemed little chance that he could find a thousand marks to pay the fine. Helpless and hopeless, he went away from the duke in the custody of a jailer.

Ægeon supposed that he knew no one in Ephesus, but at the very time he was in danger of losing his life as a result of the careful search he was making for his youngest son, both he and his brother were also in the city of Ephesus.

Besides looking exactly alike, Ægeon's sons both had the same name, Antipholus, and the two twin servants were also both named Dromio. Ægeon's younger son, Antipholus of Syracuse, happened to arrive at Ephesus, with his servant Dromio, the very

same day as Ægeon. Being a merchant of Syracuse, too, he would have been in the same danger as his father, but by good fortune, he met a friend, who told him the danger another merchant of Syracuse was in and advised him to pretend to be a merchant of Epidamnum. Antipholus agreed to do this and was sorry to hear that one of his countrymen was in this danger. He little thought, however, that this old merchant was his own father.

The elder son, who must be called Antipholus of Ephesus to distinguish him from his brother Antipholus of Syracuse, had lived in Ephesus for twenty years. He was a rich man and would have been able to pay the money for his father's life, but he knew nothing of his father. He had been so young when he and his mother were rescued from the sea by fishermen, that he remembered only that he had been rescued. He had no memory of either his father or his mother. The fishermen who rescued Antipholus, his mother and the young servant Dromio, took the two children away from her, to her great sorrow, intending to sell them as slaves.

Antipholus and Dromio were sold by the sailors to Duke Menaphon, a famous soldier, who was the Duke of Ephesus's uncle, and he took the boys to Ephesus, when he went to visit the duke.

The Duke of Ephesus took a liking to young Antipholus. When he grew up, he made him an officer in his army. Antipholus showed great bravery in the wars and saved the duke's life. The duke rewarded his courage by arranging his marriage to Adriana, a rich lady of Ephesus. Antipholus and Adriana were living in their house in Ephesus, with Dromio, their servant, still attending them, at the time his father came there.

Meanwhile, Antipholus of Syracuse had left the friend who had advised him to say he came from Epidamnum and given his servant Dromio some money to take to the inn where he intended to have dinner. In the meantime, he said, he would walk about, see the city and look at the way the people behaved.

Dromio was a jolly young man. When Antipholus was dull and miserable, Dromio used to amuse him with merry jokes, so that Dromio was allowed to be much more outspoken than is usual between masters and their servants.

After Antipholus of Syracuse had sent Dromio away, he stood for a while thinking over his solitary journeys in search of his mother and his brother. He never heard a word about them in any of the places where he landed and said sorrowfully to himself, 'I am like a drop of water in the ocean which, looking for another drop, loses itself in the wide sea. So I, unhappily, looking for my mother and brother, seem to lose myself.'

While Antipholus of Syracuse was thinking about his tedious travels, which had turned out to be so useless, Dromio apparently returned. Antipholus was surprised that he had come back so soon and asked him where he had left the money. Now, this was not his own Dromio of Syracuse but the twin brother who lived with Antipholus of Ephesus. The two Dromios and the two Antipholuses were still as much alike as Ægeon had said they were when they were babies. No wonder Antipholus thought it was his own servant who had returned. Dromio replied, 'My mistress sent me to ask you come to dinner. The chicken is burning and the pork is falling apart.'

'Now is not the time for jokes,' Antipholus said. 'Where did you leave the money?' Dromio still replied that his mistress had sent him to fetch Antipholus for dinner.

'What mistress?' said Antipholus.

'Why, sir, your wife,' replied Dromio.

Antipholus of Syracuse wasn't married, so he was very angry with Dromio, and said, 'Because I am friendly and sometimes chat with you, you take it upon yourself to joke with me in this free manner. I am not in a joking mood now. Where is the money? We are strangers here, so how dare you trust someone else to look after it?'

Dromio hearing his master, whom the thought was Antipholus of Ephesus, talk of their being strangers, supposed he was being funny. He replied merrily, 'Please, sir, joke while you sit at the dinner table. I was simply told to fetch you home, to have dinner with my mistress and her sister.'

Now Antipholus lost all patience and beat Dromio. He ran home and told his mistress that his master had refused to come to dinner and that he said he had no wife.

Adriana, Antipholus of Ephesus' wife was very angry when she heard that her husband said he was not married. She was a jealous woman and she thought that her husband meant that he loved someone else better than he loved her. She began to get worked up and say unkind and jealous things, complaining about her husband and her sister, Luciana, who lived with her, tried, without success, to persuade her out of her groundless suspicions.

Antipholus of Syracuse went to the inn and found Dromio of Syracuse with the money quite safe. He was just going to tell Dromio off for his jokes, when Adriana came up to him. She had no idea that this was not her husband and she began to complain to him that he was looking at her as though she were a stranger, as well he might, never having seen this angry lady before. Then she reminded him how much he had loved her before they were married and said that now he loved some other lady instead of her. 'How has it happened now, my husband,' she said, 'oh! how has it happened that I have lost your love?'

'Are you talking to me, madam?' said the astonished Antipholus. He could not make her believe that he was not her husband and that he had been in Ephesus only two hours. She insisted on his going home with her and Antipholus, unable to get away, finally went with her to his brother's house and dined with Adriana and her sister. One of them called him husband and the other brother. He was totally amazed and thought he must have been married to her in his sleep or that he was asleep and dreaming now. Dromio, who went with them, was just as surprised, for the cook, who was really his brother's wife, also claimed him for her husband.

While Antipholus of Syracuse was having dinner with his brother's wife, his brother, Adriana's real husband, returned home to dinner with his servant Dromio. However, the servants would not open the door because their mistress had ordered them not to let anyone in. They knocked repeatedly and said they were Antipholus and Dromio, but the maids laughed at them and said that Antipholus was at dinner with their mistress and Dromio was in the kitchen. Although they almost knocked the door down, they could not get in. Finally Antipholus went away, very angry and surprised at hearing that another man was dining with his wife.

When Antipholus of Syracuse had finished his dinner, he was still bewildered at Adriana's insisting on calling him her husband. On hearing that Dromio had also been claimed by the cook, he left the house as soon as he could find any excuse to get away. Although he liked Luciana, the sister, very much, he didn't think much of Adriana. Dromio was not very pleased with his fine wife in the kitchen either. So both master and servant were glad to get away from their new wives as fast as they could.

The moment Antipholus of Syracuse left the house, he met a goldsmith who mistook him for Antipholus of Ephesus, just as Adriana had done. The goldsmith gave him a gold chain and called him by his name. Antipholus tried to refuse the chain, saying it did not belong to him, but the goldsmith replied that he had made it on Antipholus's own orders. He went away, leaving the chain in the hands of Antipholus. He ordered Dromio to get his things on board a ship, as he did not want to stay in a place where he met with such strange adventures that he thought he must be bewitched.

The goldsmith, who had given the chain to the wrong Antipholus, was arrested immediately afterwards because he owed money. Antipholus of Ephesus, the married brother to whom the goldsmith thought he had given the chain, happened to come along just as the officer was arresting the goldsmith. When he saw Antipholus, the goldsmith asked him to pay for the gold chain he had just delivered to him, the price being nearly the same amount as he owed. Antipholus denied that he had received the chain. The goldsmith insisted that he had given it to him just a few minutes earlier. They argued for a long time, both thinking they were right. Antipholus knew that the goldsmith had never given him the chain, but because the two brothers were like each other the goldsmith was certain he had delivered the chain to him. At last the officer took the goldsmith away to prison for the debt he owed. At the same time, the goldsmith made the officer arrest Antipholus for the price of the chain. Antipholus and the goldsmith were both taken away to prison together.

As Antipholus of Ephesus was on his way to prison, he met Dromio of Syracuse, mistaking him for his own servant, he ordered him to go to Adriana, his wife, and tell her to send money for the chain. Dromio was puzzled as to why his master should send him back to the strange house where he had dinner and from which they had just hurried away. He did not dare to reply, although he had come to tell his master the ship was ready to sail, for he could see that Antipholus was in no mood for jokes. He went away, grumbling to himself that he must return to Adriana's house, 'Where,' he said,

'Dowsabel claims me for a husband. I must go, for servants must obey their master's commands.'

Adriana gave him the money. As Dromio of Syracuse was returning, he met Antipholus of Syracuse. He was still in amazement at the surprising adventures that were happening to him. His brother was well known in Ephesus, so there was hardly a man he met in the streets who didn't say hallo like an old friend. Some people offered him money, which they said they owed him; some invited him to come and see them, and some thanked him for kindnesses they said he had done them, all mistaking him for his brother. A tailor showed him some silk he had bought for him and insisted upon taking measurements for some clothes.

Antipholus began to think he was in a city of wizards and witches. Dromio did not help by asking how he got free from the officer who was taking him to prison and by giving him the purse of gold which Adriana had sent to pay the debt. This talk of Dromio's of arrest and prison and money he had brought from Adriana totally confused Antipholus. He said, 'Dromio has gone mad and we wander about here in dreams.'

Terrified at his own confused thoughts, he cried out, 'Some blessed power save us from this strange place!'

Now another stranger came up to Antipholus. She called him by his name and told him that he had dinner with her. She asked him for a gold chain which she said he had promised to give her. Antipholus now lost all patience and called her a witch. He denied that he had ever promised her a chain or dined with her or had even seen her face before now. She repeated that he had dined with her, had promised her a chain and added that she had given him a valuable ring. If he would not give her the gold chain, she wanted her own ring again. At this Antipholus became quite frantic and called her witch again. He denied all knowledge of her or her ring and ran away from her, leaving her astonished at his words and his wild looks. She was quite certain that he had dined with her and that she had given him a ring because he had promised to make her a present of a gold chain. She had fallen into the same mistake as the others, for she had taken him for his brother. The married Antipholus of Ephesus had done all the things she accused this Antipholus of Syracuse of doing.

When Antipholus of Ephesus couldn't get into his own house because everybody thought that he was already there, he had gone away very angry. He thought that this was one of his wife's jealous tantrums. She was often jealous and falsely accused him of seeing other women. He was so cross with Adriana, he decided to go and dine with this other lady. She welcomed him and because his wife had annoyed him so much, Antipholus promised to give her a gold chain which he had earlier intended to give to his wife. This was the same chain which the goldsmith, by mistake, had given to his brother. The lady liked the idea of a fine gold chain so much that she gave Antipholus of Ephesus a ring. Later he said that he had never had the ring and that he did not know her. Of course she was talking to the wrong Antipholus, but she was so cross that she began to think he was out of his mind. She decided to go and tell Adriana that her husband was mad. While she was telling all this to Adriana, Antipholus of Ephesus came home with his jailer, who allowed him to come home to get the money to pay the debt. He had returned for the purse of money which Adriana had already sent by Dromio and which he had delivered to the other Antipholus.

Adriana believed the story of her husband's madness, when he began to tell her off for shutting him out of his own house. She remembered how he had protested all through dinner that he was not her husband and had never been in Ephesus till that day. She had no doubt that he was mad. She paid the jailer the money and then ordered the servants to bind her husband with ropes. He was taken to a dark room and she sent

for a doctor to come and cure his madness. All the time Antipholus hotly exclaimed against this false accusation, which had resulted from his exact likeness to his brother. His rage only made them more sure that he was mad. Dromio insisted on the same story, so they tied him up too and took him away along with his master.

Soon after Adriana had put her husband into safe-keeping, a servant came to tell her that Antipholus and Dromio must have broken loose from their keepers, because they were both walking freely in the next street. On hearing this, Adriana ran out to fetch Antipholus home, taking some people with her to tie up her husband again. Her sister went along with her too. When they came to the gates of a nearby convent, they saw the two people, they thought were Antipholus and Dromio of Ephesus.

Antipholus of Syracuse was still very muddled. The chain which the goldsmith had given him was hanging round his neck and the goldsmith was complaining that he had denied having it and refused to pay for it. Antipholus was saying that the goldsmith gave him the chain in the morning and that he hadn't seen him since.

Now Adriana came up to him. She said that he was her mad husband who escaped from his keepers. The men she brought with her were going to grab hold of Antipholus and Dromio, but they ran into the convent. Antipholus pleaded with the abbess to give him shelter in her house.

The lady abbess herself came out to ask what was causing all the fuss. She was a serious, dignified lady and wise in understanding what she saw. She was in no hurry to give up the man who had asked for the protection of her house. She questioned Adriana about the story she told of her husband's madness and asked, 'What is the cause of this sudden problem? Has he lost all his money at sea? Or has the death of some dear friend disturbed his mind?'

Adriana replied that no such things had happened.

'Perhaps,' the abbess said, 'he has fallen in love with someone else and that has driven him to this state.' Adriana said what she had thought for a long time that the love of some other lady was why he was often away from home. Now it was not his love for another, but the nagging jealousy of his wife that often made Antipholus leave his home. The abbess suspected this because Adriana spoke so fiercely. In order to learn the truth, she said, 'You should have told him off for this.'

'I did,' Adriana replied.

'Yes,' said the abbess, 'but perhaps not enough.'

Adriana, wanting to convince the abbess that she had said enough on the subject to Antipholus, replied, 'It was all I ever talked about. I said so much about it in bed, I would not let him sleep; I said so much at mealtimes, I would not let him eat. When we were alone, I talked of nothing else, and in company I frequently hinted at it. All I ever said was how vile and bad it was of him to love someone else better than me.'

The lady abbess, having drawn this full admission from the jealous Adriana, now said, 'That's why your husband is mad. The awful nagging of a jealous woman is deadlier than being bitten by a mad dog. His sleep was spoiled by your nagging; no wonder his head is light; his meat was flavoured with your complaints; quarrelsome mealtimes are bad for the digestion and that made him ill. Your jealousy has made your husband mad.'

Luciana wanted to make excuses for her sister, saying she always complained gently to her husband and said to her sister, 'Why do you listen without answering?'

The abbess had made Adriana feel so guilty that she could only answer, 'My own words gave me away.'

Adriana, although ashamed of her own behaviour, still insisted that her husband should be returned to her care. The abbess would not let anybody enter her house, nor would she give up this unhappy man to the care of this jealous wife. She decided to use gentle means for his recovery and she went back into her house again. She ordered her gates to be shut against them.

Meanwhile, during the course of this eventful day, in which so many errors had hap-

pened as a result of the twin brothers' likeness to each other, old Ægeon's time was running out. It was nearly sunset and at sunset, he was doomed to die if he could not pay the money.

The place of execution was near the convent. He arrived there just as the abbess went back into the convent. The duke was there too so that if anyone offered to pay the money, he could immediately pardon Ægeon.

Adriana stopped this procession and asked the duke for justice. She told him that the abbess had refused to give up her mad husband to her care. While she was speaking the real husband and his servant Dromio, who had managed to get loose, came before the duke to demand justice. He complained that his wife had locked him up on a false charge of madness and described how he had broken free and escaped from his keepers. Adriana was very surprised to see her husband in the street when she thought he was inside the convent.

Ægeon, seeing Antipholus, assumed this was the son who had left him to look after his mother and his brother. He felt sure that his dear son would pay the money demanded for his fine. He spoke to Antipholus in loving words of a father and with the joyful hope that he would now be released. To his utter astonishment, his son denied all knowledge of him, as well as he might, for this Antipholus had not seen his father since they were separated in the storm when he was a baby.

Poor Ægeon was trying desperately to make his son recognize him, thinking that either his griefs and worries had altered him so much that his son did not know him, or else that he was ashamed to acknowledge his father in his misery. In the middle of all this the lady abbess and the other Antipholus and Dromio came out. Adriana saw two husbands and two Dromios standing in front of her!

Now the riddles and confusions, which had so puzzled them all, were explained. When the duke saw the two Antipholuses and the two Dromios, both so exactly alike, he immediately guessed what had happened, for he remembered the story Ægeon had told him in the morning. He said these men must be the two sons of Ægeon and their twin servants.

Now an unexpected joy completed the story of Ægeon. The tale he had told in sorrow in the morning and under sentence of death had a happy ending. The lady abbess made herself known; she was the long-lost wife of Ægeon and the loving mother of the two Antipholuses.

When the fishermen took the elder Antipholus and Dromio away from her, she entered a nunnery. Her wisdom and goodness finally made her the abbess of this convent. In caring for an unhappy stranger, she had unknowingly protected her own son.

Joyful congratulations and affectionate greetings between these long-separated parents and their children made them forget that Ægeon was still under sentence of death. When they were calmer, Antipholus of Ephesus offered the duke the fine for his father, but the duke freely pardoned Ægeon and would not take the money. He went with the abbess and her newly-found husband and children into the convent, to hear the full story of this happy family. The two Dromios must not be forgotten either. They had their congratulations and greetings too. Each Dromio told his brother how good-looking he was.

Adriana took her mother-in-law's good advice, so that she never after nursed unjust suspicions or was jealous of her husband.

Antipholus of Syracuse married Luciana, Adriana's sister and good old Ægeon lived in Ephesus many years with his wife and sons. Solving the puzzle did not remove every chance of mistakes in the future. Sometimes, to remind them of past adventures, comical blunders would happen, when one Antipholus and one Dromio would be mistaken for the other, making altogether a jolly Comedy of Errors.

Measure for Measure

In the city of Vienna there was once a duke who was so gentle and good tempered that he allowed the people to ignore the laws without getting into trouble. There was one law in particular which everybody had almost forgotten as the duke had never put it in force during his whole reign. This law stated that any man who was living with a woman who was not his wife should be put to death, but it was completely disregarded. The holy institution of marriage became neglected and every day the duke received complaints of the young girls who had been seduced from their protection and were living as the companions of single men.

The good duke saw with sadness this growing evil among his subjects, but he thought if he suddenly changed from being free and easy to being strict the people would stop loving him and consider him a tyrant. So he decided to leave Vienna for a while and put his dukedom in charge of a deputy. Then the law against these dishonourable lovers could be enforced without his seeming to be harsh.

The duke chose Angelo as his deputy. He was thought of almost as a saint in Vienna because he led such an austere life. When the duke told Lord Escalus, his chief counsellor, of his plan, Escalus said, 'If any man in Vienna is worthy of this honour, it is Lord Angelo.'

The duke left Vienna — pretending that he was making a journey into Poland — and left Angelo to act as the lord deputy in his absence. However, the duke's absence was an act, for dressed like a friar, he secretly returned to Vienna so that he could watch what the saintly-seeming Angelo did.

Just about the time that Angelo was made the duke's deputy, a man called Claudio persuaded a young woman away from her parents. At the command of the new lord deputy, Claudio was taken to prison. The old neglected law was enforced and Angelo sentenced Claudio to be beheaded. Many important people asked for young Claudio to be pardoned. The good Lord Escalus himself spoke up for him. 'Alas!' he said, 'Claudio, whom I want to save, had a respectable father. For his sake I ask you to pardon the young man's crime.'

Angelo replied, 'We must not treat the law like a scarecrow, which is set up to frighten birds of prey, until they get used to it, find it harmless and make it their perch. Sir, he must die.'

Claudio's friend, Lucio, visited him in prison and Claudio said to him, 'Please, Lucio, do this for me. Go to my sister Isabella, who is planning to enter the convent of Saint Clare today and tell her of the danger I am in. Ask her to make friends with the strict deputy; beg her to go to Angelo herself. I have great hopes in that, for she is very persuasive and her sadness may change his mind.'

Isabella, Claudio's sister, had, as he said, begun her training as nun that day. She was asking a nun about the rules of the convent, when they heard the voice of Lucio. When he entered the convent, he said, 'Peace be in this place!'

'Who is that?' asked Isabella.

'It is a man's voice,' the nun replied. 'Isabella, go and find out what he wants. You may but I am not allowed. When you have become a nun, you must not speak to men except in the presence of the prioress. Then if you speak you must not show your face, or if you show your face, you must not speak.'

'And have you nuns no other privileges?' Isabella asked.

'Are these not enough?' replied the nun.

'Yes, truly,' Isabella said, 'I did not mean I wanted more, but rather that I wished the sisterhood was even stricter.'

They heard the voice of Lucio again, and the nun said, 'He calls out again, please answer him.' Isabella then went out to Lucio and asked who he was. Lucio approaching with respect, said, 'Can you take me to see Isabella, a novice of this convent and the sister to the unhappy Claudio?'

'Why is he unhappy?' Isabella said. 'Tell me, for I am Isabella, his sister.'

'Madam,' he replied, 'your brother sends his best wishes but he is in prison.'

'Oh no! What for?' Isabella said. Lucio then told her Claudio was imprisoned for seducing a young girl. 'Ah,' she said, 'I am afraid it is my friend Juliet.' Juliet and Isabella had been friends when they were at school and Isabella knew that Juliet loved Claudio, so she feared that she had been led astray by her affection for him.

'Yes, it is Juliet,' Lucio replied.

'Why then my brother can marry Juliet,' Isabella said.

Lucio replied that Claudio would gladly marry Juliet but that the lord deputy had sentenced him to death for this offence. 'Unless,' he said, 'you have the grace to soften Angelo's heart. That is why I have come to see you.'

'Oh, dear!' Isabella said, 'I don't think I can do him much good. I doubt I have any power to move Angelo.'

'Our doubts are like traitors,' said Lucio, 'if they make us lose the good we might win, if we are afraid to try. Go to Lord Angelo! When women ask for help and kneel and cry, men give as generously as gods.'

'I will see what I can do,' said Isabella. 'I will just tell the prioress what has happened and then I will go to Angelo. Give my love to my brother. Soon I will send him news of my success.'

Isabella hurried to the palace and threw herself on her knees before Angelo, saying, 'I am a miserable petitioner, please listen to me.'

'Well, what do you want?' Angelo asked. Then in the most moving words she begged for her brother's life.

Unmoved, Angelo said, 'There is no hope. Your brother has been sentenced and he must die.'

'It is just a law but very severe!' said Isabella. 'I *had* a brother then — goodbye!'

She was about to leave, but Lucio, who had gone with her, said, 'Do not give up. Go back to him — beg him, kneel down before him, grab hold of his robe. You are too calm — you sound as if you are doing the shopping.' Once more Isabella on her knees begged for mercy.

'He has been sentenced,' Angelo said. 'It is too late.'

'Too late!' said Isabella. 'No it isn't. Anyone can take back their words. Believe this, my lord, none of the symbols of important people — not the king's crown, the deputy's sword, the marshal's truncheon, or the judge's robe — suits them as much as mercy does.'

'Please go,' said Angelo.

Isabella still pleaded with him, 'If my brother had been in your shoes and you in his, you might have slipped into bad behaviour like him, but he would not have been so stern a judge as you. I wish I had your power and you were Isabella. Things would be different then. I would tell you what it means to be a judge and what a prisoner.'

'That's enough,' Angelo said. 'It is the law, not I, that condemns your brother. Even if he were my own brother, or my son, it would still be the same. He must die tomorrow.'

'Tomorrow?' Isabella said. 'Oh, that is sudden! Spare him, spare him! He is not prepared for death. My lord, think — no one else has died for my brother's crime, although many have committed it. So you would be the first judge to give this sentence and he the first person that suffers it. Look into your own heart, my lord, and ask if it has ever had the same thoughts as my brother's. If it admits such thoughts, it should not allow a thought against my brother's life.' Her last words affected Angelo more than everything else she had said, for Isabella's beauty had stirred a guilty passion in his heart. He began to form thoughts of dishonourable love just as Claudio's crime had been. The confusion in his mind made him turn away from Isabella, but she called him back, saying, 'My lord, turn back. Listen to how I will bribe you. Turn back.' 'What do you mean, bribe me!' Angelo said, astonished that she should think of offering a bribe.

'Yes,' Isabella said, 'with such gifts that Heaven itself share with you. Not with golden treasures or glittering jewels which are only valuable when they are fashionable, but with true prayers that shall reach to Heaven before sunrise — prayers from women and girls who have turned their backs on the world and dedicated their lives to God.'

'Well, come and see me tomorrow,' Angelo said. This short delay and permission to be heard again gave Isabella hope that she might at last overcome his stern nature. As she went away she said, 'Heaven keep you safe! Heaven save you!'

When Angelo heard this, he said within his heart, 'Amen! I want to be saved from you and from your goodness.' Frightened by his own evil thoughts, he added, 'What is this? What is this? Do I love her, that I long to hear her speak again and to see her beauty? What is it I am dreaming of? The devil is cunning; when he wants to catch a saint, he traps him with another saint. A bad woman could not begin to stir my feelings, but this good woman has completely won me over. Until now I never understood why people fell in love.'

The guilty battle going on in his mind made Angelo suffer more that night than the prisoner he had so severely sentenced. In prison, Claudio was visited by the good duke, who in his friar's clothing taught the young man the way to Heaven, preaching to him the words of penitence and peace. However, Angelo felt pangs of guilt and could not make up his mind. First he wanted to seduce Isabella from the path of innocence and goodness, and then he was full of remorse and horror for a crime which was still only in his imagination. In the end his evil thoughts won. He, who had been horrified at the offer of a bribe, decided to tempt Isabella with a bribe she could not turn down — the precious gift of her dear brother's life.

In the morning, Angelo ordered Isabella to be admitted alone to his presence. When she came in he told her that if she would agree to a dishonourable liaison with him just as Juliet had with Claudio, he would give her her brother's life. 'For,' he said, 'I love you, Isabella.'

'My brother,' Isabella replied, 'loves Juliet and yet you tell me he must die for it.'

'But,' Angelo said, 'Claudio shall not die if you will agree to meet me secretly at night, just as Juliet left her father's house at night to come to Claudio.'

Isabella was amazed that he should try to make her to do the same thing that had caused him to pass a sentence of death upon her brother. She said, 'I would rather die than give myself up to this shame.' Then she told him that she hoped he spoke these words only to test her.

He said, 'Believe me, on my honour, I mean just what I say.'

Isabella, furious at hearing him use the word honour to express such a dishonourable purpose, said, 'You have little honour for me to believe! I will tell everyone about you, Angelo. Sign a pardon for my brother immediately or I will tell the world aloud what sort of man you are!'

'Who will believe you, Isabella?' Angelo said. 'My reputation, the strictness of my life, my word against yours, will outweigh your accusation. Save your brother by doing what I ask or he will die tomorrow. As for you, say what you can, my lies will outweigh your true story. Answer me tomorrow.'

'Who can I complain to? Who would believe me?' Isabella said when she went towards the dreary prison where her brother was locked up. When she arrived there, she found her brother in pious conversation with the duke, still in his friar's habit. He had also visited Juliet and brought both these guilty lovers to a proper sense of their fault. Juliet, with tears and feeling truly sorry, admitted that she was more to blame than Claudio because she willingly agreed to his dishonourable request.

Isabella entered the room where Claudio was imprisoned. 'Who is there?' said the disguised duke. 'Come in.'

'I must have a word or two with Claudio,' Isabella said. The duke left them together but asked the provost who had the charge of the prisoners to find him a place where he could overhear their conversation.

'Now, sister, can you offer me any comfort?' Claudio asked. Isabella told him that he must prepare for death the next day. 'Is there no way to save me?' Claudio said.

'Yes, brother,' Isabella replied, 'there is. But it is a way that, if you agreed to it, would strip your honour from you.'

'Tell me,' Claudio said.

'Oh, I am afraid of you, Claudio,' his sister replied. 'I am afraid that you care more about adding a few brief years to your life than your honour. Do you dare to die?'

'Why are you trying to make me ashamed?' Claudio said. 'If I must die, I will meet the darkness of death as if it were a bride and hug it in my arms.'

'There spoke my brother,' Isabella said. 'That was the voice of our family honour. Yes, you must die. Yet — would you believe it, Claudio — this deputy who everyone thinks is a saint, would pardon you if I agree with a dishonourable liaison with him. Oh, if he wanted my life, I would die for your safety without a second thought!'

'Thanks, dear Isabella,' Claudio said.

'Be ready to die tomorrow,' said Isabella.

'Death is a fearful thing,' Claudio said.

'And a shamed life is a hateful thing,' his sister replied.

Thoughts of death now overcame Claudio's feelings and in terror he cried out, 'Sweet sister, let me live! Because you would be doing it to save a brother's life, the sin would stop being a sin and become a good deed.'

'O faithless coward! O dishonest wretch!' Isabella said. 'Would you save your life by paying for it with your sister's shame? I thought that you were so full of honour that even if you had twenty heads to be cut off, you would have given them all up before you allowed your sister to stoop to such dishonour.'

'No, listen to me, Isabella!' said the agonized Claudio.

What he would have said in defence of his weakness in wanting to live at the expense of his good sister, was interrupted by the entrance of the duke, who said, 'Claudio, I have overheard what you and your sister have said. Angelo never meant to corrupt her, he was only testing her. She having the truth of honour in her, said no and he was glad to hear it. There is no hope that he will pardon you, so pass your hours in prayer and make ready for death.'

Claudio was sorry for his weakness and said, 'Let me ask my sister's pardon. I am so out of love with life that I will ask to be rid of it.' Claudio went away, overwhelmed with shame and sorrow for his fault.

The duke being now alone with Isabella praised her goodness and strength of mind, saying, 'You are as good as you are beautiful.'

'Oh,' Isabella said, 'the good duke is deceived by Angelo! If he ever comes back and I can speak to him, I will tell him how Angelo ruled.' Isabella did not know that she was telling the duke at that very moment.

The duke replied, 'That will be a great thing, but as the matter now stands, Angelo will deny your accusation, so listen to my advice. I believe that you may help a poor wronged woman and save your brother without doing any harm to your own beliefs. You will also please the duke, if by any chance he ever returns to hear of this business.' Isabella said she was brave enough to do anything he wanted, provided it was nothing wrong. 'Goodness is brave,' said the duke. Then he asked her if she had ever heard of Mariana, the sister of Frederick, a great soldier who had been drowned at sea.

'I have heard of the lady,' Isabella said, 'and good words went with her name.'

The duke said, 'Mariana is Angelo's wife but her marriage dowry was on board the ship which sank, drowning her brother. Poor woman, this was extra bad luck. She lost her most noble and famous brother, who had always loved her and, in the loss of her riches, she lost the love of her husband. Angelo pretended to discover some shameful story about this honourable lady, although the true cause was the loss of her dowry, and left her in her tears. His unfair unkindness should have stopped her love for him but Mariana only loves him more.'

The duke then told Isabella his plan. She was to go to Lord Angelo and apparently agree to meet him, as he wanted, at midnight. By this means she would obtain the promised pardon for Claudio. However, Mariana would meet Angelo in her stead and pretend to be Isabella. 'Nor, gentle daughter,' said the pretend friar, 'should you be worried about doing this. Angelo is her husband and to bring them together is not wrong.'

Isabella was pleased with this plan and went off to do as he told her. He went to tell Mariana. He had already visited her in his pretend character to give her religious instruction and friendly comfort. It was on these visits that he had learned her sad story from her own lips. Now, looking upon him as a holy man, she readily agreed to be directed by him in this undertaking.

Isabella had arranged to meet the duke at Mariana's house after she had been to see Angelo. When she arrived, he said, 'I'm glad you're here so promptly! What is the news about Angelo?'

Isabella told him how she had settled things. 'Angelo,' she said, 'has a garden with a brick wall round it, on the western side there is a gate into a vineyard.' Then she showed the duke and Mariana two keys that Angelo had given to her. She said, 'This bigger key opens the vineyard gate, this other a little door which leads from the vine-

yard to the garden. I have promised to meet him there at the dead of night and he has promised to pardon my brother. I have taken a careful note of the place which he explained to me in whispers twice over.'

'Are there no other signs that you agreed with him that Mariana must remember?' asked the duke.

'No, none,' said Isabella, 'only to go when it is dark. I have told him that I won't have much time for I have made him think a servant will come along with me and that this servant believes I am going to see him about my brother.'

The duke praised her discreet management. Turning to Mariana, she said, 'You don't have to say much to Angelo when you leave him, except to whisper *Remember now my brother!*'

Isabella took Mariana to the meeting place that night. She was happy that she had, as she supposed, saved her brother's life and her own honour by this trick. However, the duke was not so sure of Claudio's life, so at midnight he went to the prison again. It was lucky for Claudio that he did because otherwise he would have been beheaded that night. Soon after the duke entered the prison, an order came from the cruel deputy that Claudio should be beheaded and his head sent to him by five o'clock in the morning. The duke persuaded the provost to put off the execution and to deceive Angelo by sending him the head of a man who had died that morning in the prison. The provost still thought the duke was an ordinary friar, so to persuade him to agree to this, the duke showed him a letter written in the duke's own handwriting and sealed with his seal. When the provost saw this, he concluded that the friar must have secret orders from the absent duke and agreed to spare Claudio. He cut off the dead man's head and sent it to Angelo.

Then the duke wrote Angelo a letter, saying that an accident had put stop to his journey and that he would be in Vienna by the following morning. He told Angelo to meet him at the entrance to the city, where he was to give up his authority as deputy. The duke also ordered Angelo to announce that if any of his subjects wanted wrongs put right, they should show their requests in the street on his first entrance into the city.

Early in the morning Isabella came to the prison. The duke was waiting for her. He had further plans so he was going to tell that Claudio had been beheaded. Isabella asked if Angelo had sent the pardon for her brother. The duke replied, 'Angelo has released Claudio from this world. His head is off and has been sent to the deputy.'

Heartbroken Isabella cried out, 'O, unhappy Claudio, wretched Isabella, cruel world, most wicked Angelo!' The pretend friar comforted her and when she became a little calmer, he told her that the duke was about to return and advised her how to bring her complaint against Angelo. He also told her not to worry if the case seemed to go against her for a while. Next the duke went to Mariana and advised her what to do.

Then the duke took off his friar's habit and put on his own royal robes. A joyful crowd of faithful subjects had assembled to greet his arrival. He entered the city of Vienna, where he was met by Angelo, who gave up his authority as deputy in the proper way. Isabella came to the duke as a petitioner for justice and said, 'Justice, most royal duke! I am a sister of Claudio. He was condemned to lose his head as a punishment for seducing a young girl. I asked Lord Angelo for my brother's pardon. It is not necessary to tell your Grace how I begged and kneeled, how he refused me and how

I replied, for this took a long time, but with grief and shame I will tell you the result. Angelo refused to release my brother unless I accepted his dishonourable love. I argued what to do within myself and finally my sisterly love overcame my belief in doing right and I gave in to him. Next morning, Angelo broke his promise and sent a warrant for my poor brother's head!'

The duke pretended not to believe her story and Angelo said that grief over her brother's death, which was entirely according to the law, had disordered her mind.

Now another person looking for justice approached. This was Mariana and she said, 'Noble prince, as light comes from heaven and truth from breath, as there is sense in truth and truth in goodness, I am this man's wife. The words of Isabella are false, for the night she says she was with Angelo, I spent with him in the garden-house. If I am lying, may I be fixed here like a marble statue forever.'

Isabella then asked for Friar Lodowick to witness that she told the truth. That was the name the duke had taken in his disguise. Isabella and Mariana had both obeyed his instructions in what they had said. The duke planned that Isabella's innocence should be proved in public before the whole city of Vienna. Angelo did not know why their stories were different and he hoped that the muddle would enable him to clear himself from Isabella's accusation. Assuming a look of offended innocence, he said, 'I thought this was just silliness but now I am beginning to get annoyed. These poor mad women are but the instruments of some more important person who sets them on. Let me find out who.'

'Yes, with all my heart,' said the duke, 'and punish him as much as you like. You, Lord Escalus, sit with Lord Angelo and help him to discover the truth. I have sent for the friar who set them on. When he comes, punish him for making these women harm your reputation in the way you think best. I must leave you for a while, but you, Lord Angelo, must stay till you have decided about this slander.'

The duke then went away, leaving Angelo pleased to be put in charge of judging his own cause. However, the duke was gone only long enough to take off his royal robes and put on his friar's habit. In that disguise he again presented himself before Angelo and Escalus. The good old Escalus, who thought Angelo had been falsely accused, said to the supposed friar, 'Come, sir, you set these women on to slander Lord Angelo?'

He replied, 'Where is the duke? He should be here to hear me speak.'

Escalus said, 'The duke's power is in us and we will hear you. Speak justly.'

'Boldly at least,' retorted the friar. Then he blamed the duke for leaving Isabella's case in the hands of the very man she had accused. Then he spoke so freely of the many bad and cheating things he had noticed while he had been in Vienna, that Escalus threatened him with torture for speaking against the state and for criticizing the behaviour of the duke. He ordered him to be taken to prison. Then, to everyone's amazement, and to the utter confusion of Angelo, the pretend friar took off his disguise and they saw he was the duke himself.

First the duke spoke to Isabella. He said to her, 'Come here, Isabella. Your friar is now your prince, but I have not changed any feelings just because I have changed my clothes. I am still devoted to your service.'

'Oh, forgive me,' said Isabella, 'that I who am your subject have employed and troubled you without knowing.'

He answered that he had more need of forgiveness from her for not having prevented the death of her brother. He would not yet tell her that Claudio was living, because he intended a further test of her goodness. Angelo now knew that the duke had been a secret witness of his bad deeds. He said, 'O my lord, I should be even guiltier if I tried to pretend that these things didn't happen when I know that you, like God himself, have seen everything I've done. Good prince, do not make my shame any greater, but let my trial be my own admission. Immediate sentence and death is all I ask.'

The duke replied, 'Angelo, your faults are obvious. I condemn you to the very block where Claudio knelt to death and with the same speed. As for his possessions, Mariana, I give them all to you as his widow so that you can buy yourself a better husband.'

'O my dear lord,' said Mariana, 'I do not want another husband or a better man.' On her knees, just as Isabella had begged for the life of Claudio, the kind wife of this ungrateful husband begged for the life of Angelo. She said, 'My lord duke, O my lord! Sweet Isabella, take my side! Kneel with me now and I will be grateful for the rest of my life.'

The duke said, 'It is against all sense for you to ask Isabella to plead for Angelo. If she were to kneel down to beg for mercy, her brother's ghost would break his gravestone and take her away in horror.'

Mariana still said, 'Isabella, sweet Isabella, just kneel by me, hold up your hand and say nothing — I will speak. They say the best men are moulded out of faults and become much the better for having been a little bad. So may my husband. O, Isabella, will you not kneel?'

The duke then said, 'He dies for Claudio.'

Then, to his delight Isabella, whom he loved and from whom he expected gracious and honourable behaviour, kneeled down before him. She said, 'Most generous sir, please consider this condemned man as if my brother lived. I partly think a true sense of duty controlled his actions, till he saw me. If this is the case, do not let him die! My brother had only justice in that he did actually do the wrong for which he died.'

The best reply the duke could make to this woman who generously asked for her enemy's life was to send for Claudio, who was still in prison, unsure of his future. He said to Isabella, 'Give me your hand, Isabella. For your lovely sake I pardon Claudio. Say you will marry me and he shall be my brother too.' By this time, Lord Angelo realized he was safe. The duke, noticing that he had brightened up a little, said, 'Well, Angelo, see to it that you love your wife. Her goodness has obtained your pardon. I wish you happiness, Mariana! Love her, Angelo! I know what a good woman she is.' Angelo remembered how hard his heart had been when he was the duke's deputy and realized how sweet mercy is.

The duke ordered Claudio to marry Juliet, and again asked Isabella to marry him. As she had not yet become a nun, she was free to marry. The duke had been so kind to her while he was disguised as a humble friar, she accepted the honour he offered her with thanks and joy. When she became Duchess of Vienna, her excellent example of good behaviour and honour stopped the young women of the city ever falling into the wrongdoing of Juliet, the repentant wife of the reformed Claudio. So the mercy-loving duke reigned for a long time with his beloved Isabella and was happiest of husbands and of princes.

Twelfth Night

Sebastian and his sister Viola, who came from Messaline, were twins. They looked so like each other that, if it weren't for their clothes, they could not be told apart. They had both been born in the same hour and now they were both in danger of dying in the same hour for they were shipwrecked off the coast of Illyria. The ship on which they were travelling, had split on a rock in a violent storm and a very small number of the crew escaped with their lives. The captain and a few of the sailors managed to reach land in a small boat. They brought Viola safe to shore with them. Once there, instead of rejoicing at her own safety, she began to grieve over her brother's loss, but the captain comforted her. He said he had seen her brother tie himself to a strong mast when the ship broke up. As long as he was able to see anything of him, he was still floating on the waves. Viola was much comforted by the hope this account gave her and now considered what she should do in a strange country so far from home. She asked the captain if he knew anything of Illyria.

'Yes, very well, madam,' the captain replied, 'for I was born no more than three hours' travel from this place.'

'Who is the ruler here?' Viola asked. The captain told her that Illyria was governed by Orsino, who was a noble duke and a fine man. Viola said she had heard her father speak of this Orsino and that he was unmarried then. 'And he is so now,' replied the captain, 'or was until recently. I left here only a month ago and then the gossip was that Orsino was in love with Olivia, the daughter of a count who died a year ago. She was left in the protection of her brother, who shortly after also died. They say that for love of him she has shut herself away from the sight and company of men.'

Viola, who was herself grief-stricken over her brother's loss, wished she could live with this lady who so mourned her brother's death. She asked the captain if he could introduce her to Olivia, whom she would willingly serve. He replied this would be difficult to do because Lady Olivia would not admit anyone to her house since her brother's death, not even the duke himself. Then Viola formed another project. She decided to dress up as a man to serve the Duke Orsino as a page. It was an odd idea for a young lady to put on men's clothes and pretend to be a boy, but given that Viola was young and very beautiful and that she had no one to protect and care for her in this foreign country, it made sense.

The captain had been kind and showed a friendly interest in her welfare, so she told him her plan. He readily agreed to help her. Viola gave him some money and asked him to buy her some suitable clothes in the same colour and the same fashion as her brother Sebastian used to wear. When she was dressed in her new outfit, she looked exactly like her brother.

After he had transformed her into a man, Viola's good friend, the captain, arranged for her to be presented to Orsino under the name of Cesario. The duke was very pleased with the way this handsome young man spoke and behaved and made Cesario one of his pages. She did her new job so well and showed such a willingness and loyalty that she soon became his most favourite attendant. Orsino told Cesario the whole story of his love for Lady Olivia. He explained how he had tried and failed to make her love him and how she now refused to admit him to her presence. For love of this lady, who had treated him so unkindly, Orsino had given up the sports and manly hobbies that he used to love and spent his time doing nothing and listening to soft music and love songs. He neglected the wise and knowledgeable lords with whom he used to associate and now spent all day in long conversing with young Cesario. No doubt his serious courtiers thought Cesario was an unsuitable companion for their once noble master, the great Duke Orsino.

It is a risky matter for young girls to become close friends of handsome young dukes. Viola found this out all too soon, for all the things Orsino had told her he endured for Olivia, she began to recognize in herself. She was suffering for the love of him. She could not understand how Olivia could be so indifferent to her wonderful lord and master for she thought no one could see him without feeling the deepest admiration. Gently she hinted to Orsino that it was a pity that he should fall in love with someone who was so blind to his good qualities. She said, 'Supposing a lady were to love you, my lord, as you love Olivia — and perhaps there is one who does — and supposing you could not love her in return would you not tell her so? Wouldn't she have to be satisfied with that answer?' Orsino would not listen to this argument, for he denied that it was possible for any woman to love as much as he did. He said no woman's heart was big enough to hold so much love, so it was unfair to compare a lady's love of him to his love for Olivia. Now, although Viola had great respect for the duke's opinions, she could not help thinking this was not quite true. She thought her heart had as much love in it as Orsino's had and she said, 'Ah! but I know, my lord . . .'

'What do you know, Cesario?' asked Orsino.

'I know too well,' Viola replied, 'what love women may have for men. They are as true of heart as we are. My father had a daughter who loved a man as I, if I were a woman, should love your lordship.'

'What is her story?' Orsino asked.

'A blank, my lord,' Viola replied. 'She never told her love, but let secret eat away, like a worm in the bud, at her rosy cheek. She pined and sat like Patience on a monument, smiling at Grief.'

The duke asked if this lady died of her love, but Viola didn't answer yes or no.

While they were talking, a man whom the duke had sent to Olivia came in. He said, 'My lord, I was not allowed to see the lady, but she sent an answer by her handmaid.' She said, 'Until seven years have passed, even the weather shall not see her face. Like a nun she will walk veiled, watering her room with her tears for the sad memory of her dead brother.'

On hearing this the duke exclaimed, 'Oh! she has a fine heart to pay this debt of love to a dead brother. How much will she love, when she finally falls in love!' Then he said to Viola, 'You know, Cesario, I have told you all the secrets of my heart. Go to Olivia's

house. Do not let them refuse to let you in. Stand at her door and tell her there your foot shall grow fixed till you see her.'

'If I do speak to her, my lord, what then?' Viola asked.

'Oh, then,' Orsino replied, 'tell her how much I love her. Make a long speech to her of my loyalty. You are a good choice for this task because she will listen more to you than to someone more serious looking.'

Viola went, but she was not very willing to try to persuade a lady to become the wife of the very man she wished to marry herself. However, having agreed to do as she was asked, she did it faithfully. Olivia soon heard that there was a young man at her door who insisted upon being allowed to see her. 'I told him,' the servant said, 'that you were ill; he said he knew you were and that was why he came to speak to you. I told him that you were asleep; he seemed to know that too and said that that was why he must speak to you. What shall I say to him, madam? He seems to stand firm against all refusals and will speak to you, whether you want to or not.'

Olivia, curious to see this bossy messenger, ordered the servant to let him in. Covering her face with her veil, she said that she would once more hear Orsino's request, as she had no doubt that he came from the duke. Viola came in, putting on the manliest swagger she could manage and spoke in fine courtier's words. She said to the veiled lady, 'Most radiant, exquisite and matchless beauty, please tell me if you are the lady of the house, for I should be sorry to waste my speech on the wrong person. Apart from the fact that it is excellently written, and I have taken great trouble to learn it.'

'Where do you come from, sir?' Olivia asked.

'I can say little more than I have learned by heart,' replied Viola, 'and that question is not written in my script.'

'Are you a comedian?' said Olivia.

'No,' Viola replied. 'Yet I am not what I seem.' Again she asked Olivia if she were the lady of the house. Olivia said she was. Then Viola, more curious about her rival's looks than eager to deliver her master's message, said, 'Madam, let me see your face.' Olivia was happy to raise her veil for this haughty beauty, whom the Duke Orsino had loved for so long, had fallen in love at first sight with the supposed page, the humble Cesario.

When Viola asked to see her face, Olivia said, 'Have you orders from your lord and master to talk to my face?' Then forgetting her determination to keep veiled for seven long years, she raised it, saying, 'But I will draw the curtain and show the picture. Is it well done?'

Viola replied, 'It is real beauty. Nature's own clever hand has painted the red and white upon your cheeks. You are the cruellest lady living if you will leave these graces to the grave and leave the world no copy.'

'Oh, sir,' Olivia replied, 'I will not be so cruel. The world may have a list of my beauty. As, *item*, two lips, ordinary red, *item*, two grey eyes with lids to them, one neck, one chin and so on. Were you sent here to praise me?'

Viola replied, 'I see what sort of person you are. You are too proud, but you are very beautiful. My lord and master loves you. Orsino loves you with adoration and with tears, with groans that thunder love and sight of fire.'

'Your lord,' Olivia said, 'knows my mind. I cannot love him, though I have no doubt that he is a good man. I know he is noble and of a good family and in the prime of life. Everyone describes him as learned, polite and brave, but I cannot love him. He should have accepted this answer long ago.'

'If I loved you as my master does,' Viola said, 'I would build a willow cabin at your gates and call out your name. I would write loving poems about Olivia and sing them in the dead of the night. Your name should sound among the hills and I would make Echo, the babbling voice of the air, cry out, Olivia! Oh, you would not be able to live without pitying me.'

'You might do much,' Olivia said. 'Who were your parents?'

Viola replied, 'Above my fortunes, but my state is still good. I am a gentleman.'

Olivia now reluctantly sent Viola away, saying, 'Go to your master and tell him that I cannot love him. He must send no more messengers, unless perhaps you come again to tell me how he takes it.'

Viola left, calling Olivia Fair Cruelty as she said goodbye. When she had gone, Olivia repeated the words, *Above my fortunes, but my state is still good. I am a gentleman.* She said aloud, 'I am sure he is; his looks, words and actions plainly show he is a gentleman.' She wished that Cesario were a duke and then realizing how firmly he had taken hold of her affections, she told herself off for her sudden love. However, when people tell themselves off, they are usually gentle about it and don't take much notice, so soon the noble Lady Olivia forgot the inequality between her fortunes and those of the page, Cesario. She decided to persuade Cesario to fall in love with her and sent a servant after him with a diamond ring that she pretended he had left with her as a present from Orsino. She hoped by making Cesario a present of the ring, she would be giving him a clue about her plan. Indeed, it did make Viola suspicious because she knew that Orsino had not sent a ring and she began to remember that Olivia's looks and behaviour had suggested a liking for her. She soon guessed that Olivia had fallen in love with her. 'Oh, dear,' she said, 'the poor lady might as well love a dream.'

Viola returned to Orsino's palace and told him of her failure, repeating Olivia's command that the duke should stop bothering her. The duke, however, hoped that gentle Cesario would in time be able to persuade her to show some pity, so he told him to go to her again the next day. In the meantime, to pass away the tedious interval, he ordered a song which he loved to be sung. He said, 'My good Cesario, when I heard that song last night, it seemed to soothe my feelings. Listen to it, Cesario, it is old and plain. Old women knitting in the sun and young girls weaving chant this song. It is silly, yet I love it because it tells of the innocence of love in the old times.'

SONG

Come away, come away, Death!
And in sad cypress let me be laid;
Fly away, fly away, breath!
I am slain by a fair cruel maid.
My shroud of white, stuck all with yew,
Oh, prepare it!
My part of death, no one so true
Did share it.
Not a flower, not a flower sweet,
On my black coffin let there be strown;
Not a friend, not a friend greet
My poor corpse, where my bones shall be thrown;
A thousand thousand sighs to save,
Lay me, O, where
Sad true lover never find my grave,
To weep there!

Viola did not fail to take notice of the words of the old song, which described so simply the pain of loving someone who doesn't love you. Her own inner feelings showed in her face and, noticing that she looked sad, Orsino said, 'I believe I know the truth, Cesario. Though you are so young, you have fallen in love, haven't you, boy?'

'A little,' Viola replied.

'What kind of woman and how old is she?' Orsino asked.

'Your age and your colouring, my lord,' said Viola. It made the duke smile to hear this fair young boy say that he loved a woman so much older than himself and with a man's dark colouring. Of course Viola secretly meant Orsino himself and not a woman like him.

When Viola visited Olivia again, she found no difficulty in being allowed in. The instant she arrived, the gates were thrown wide open and the duke's page was shown into Olivia's apartment with great respect. When Viola told her that she had come to speak on her lord's behalf once more, Olivia said, 'I asked you never to speak of him again. However, I had rather hear you speak of love yourself.' This was pretty plain speaking, but Olivia soon explained herself still more plainly. She openly admitted that she was in love with Cesario and when she saw Viola look worried and unhappy, she said, 'Oh, how handsome you look when you are angry! Cesario, I love you so much that, in spite of your pride, I am not clever enough to hide my feelings.' Poor Olivia was wasting her breath. Viola hurried from her, threatening that she would never come again to speak of Orsino's love. The only reply she made to Olivia's fond appeals was the promise never to love any woman.

No sooner had Viola left the lady than she was faced with another problem. A knight called Sir Andrew Aguecheek had asked Olivia to marry him and she had turned him down. He had learned how that lady favoured the duke's messenger and challenged him to fight a duel. What on earth could poor Viola do? Although she looked like a man, she had absolutely no idea how to fight with a sword.

When she saw her rival advancing towards her with his sword drawn, she began to think of admitting that she was a woman, but all of a sudden she was rescued from her terror and shame of such discovery, by a stranger. He spoke to her as if they were old friends and said to Sir Andrew, 'If this young gentleman offended you, I will take the fault on me; and if you offend him, I will defy you for his sake.'

Before Viola had time to thank him for his protection or to ask the reason for his kind interference, her new friend met with an enemy where his bravery was of no use to him. At that very moment, officers of the law came along and arrested the stranger in

the duke's name to answer for an offence he had committed some years before. He said to Viola, 'This comes from looking for you.' Then he asked her for his purse, saying, 'Now I have to ask for my purse. I am much more upset about not being able to help you, than about what has happened to me. You look surprised. Never mind, cheer up.'

His words did indeed surprise Viola and she told him that she didn't know him and had never received a purse from him. As he had just shown her such kindness, she offered him a small sum of money, that being nearly all she had. Now, the stranger accused her of ingratitude and unkindness. He said, 'I snatched this young man from the jaws of death. I only came to Illyria for his sake and have now fallen into this danger.'

The law officers cared little for the complaints of their prisoner and they hurried him off, saying, 'What is that to us?' As he was taken away, he called Viola by the name of Sebastian, reproaching him for disowning his friend for as long as he was within hearing. When Viola heard herself called Sebastian, she began to wonder whether this mystery had arisen from her being mistaken for her brother. She also began to hope that it was her brother whose life this man said he had saved. This is exactly what had happened. The stranger, whose name was Antonio, was a sea captain. He had taken Sebastian on board his ship during the storm which had wrecked the ship that the twins had been travelling on. He and Sebastian had become such good friends that he decided to go with Sebastian wherever he went. Sebastian decided to visit Orsino's court and Antonio, rather than part from him, came to Illyria, although he knew that his life would be in danger because he had once dangerously wounded the duke's nephew in a sea-fight. This was why he had now been arrested.

Antonio and Sebastian had landed together only a few hours before Antonio met Viola. He had given his purse to Sebastian, and told him to use the money freely if he saw anything he wanted to buy. Antonio waited for his young friend at the inn, while Sebastian went to look at the town. When Sebastian did not return at the time they had agreed, Antonio went out to look for him. When he saw Viola, who was dressed in the same way and who looked exactly like her brother, Antonio drew his sword in, as he supposed, Sebastian's defence. When Sebastian apparently disowned him and denied having had his purse, it is no wonder he accused him of ingratitude.

When Antonio was gone, Viola, fearing a second invitation to fight, hurried home as fast as she could. She had not been long gone, when Sir Andrew thought he saw her return, but it was in fact Sebastian who happened to arrive at this place. Sir Andrew said, 'Now, sir, have I met with you again? There's for you!' and he hit Sebastian. Sebastian was no coward. He hit him back and drew his sword.

Just at this moment, Olivia came out of the house and she, too, mistook Sebastian for Cesario. She invited him to come in and expressed much sorrow at the rude attack he had met with. Sebastian was as much surprised at the politeness of the lady as at the rudeness of his unknown enemy, but he went with her very willingly. Olivia was then delighted to find that Cesario, as she thought, had become more responsive to her attentions. Sebastian did not at all object to the way Olivia treated him. He seemed to take it in very good part, although he wondered quite what was going on and was rather inclined to think Olivia was not in her right senses. However, realizing that she was the owner of a fine house and that she organized herself and her family sensibly and that, apart from her sudden love for him, she appeared in the full possession of her reason, he approved of the talk of love. Olivia, finding Cesario in this good mood and fearing that he might change his mind, suggested that, as she had a priest in the house, they should be married at once. Sebastian agreed to this proposal. When the wedding was over, he left his lady for a short time, intending to go and tell his friend Antonio the good news.

In the meantime, Orsino came to visit Olivia and just as he reached Olivia's house, the officers of the law brought their prisoner Antonio along. Viola was with Orsino and when Antonio saw her, still thinking she was Sebastian, he told the duke how he had rescued this young man from the danger of the sea. After telling the full story of all the kindness he had shown to Sebastian, he ended by saying that for three months, both day and night, this ungrateful boy had been with him. However, as the Lady Olivia was coming out of her house, the duke could no longer attend to Antonio's story and he said, 'Here comes the countess: now heaven walks on earth! As for you, my good man, your words are madness. This boy has been my page for three months.' He then ordered Antonio to be taken aside. Orsino's heavenly countess soon gave the duke cause to accuse Cesario as much of ingratitude as Antonio had done. The only words Olivia spoke were words of kindness to Cesario. When Orsino found that his page had obtained this high place in Olivia's favour, he threatened him with all sorts of terrors. He was about to go and called Viola to follow him, saying, 'Come, boy, with me. My thoughts are ripe for trouble.' It looked as though he might end up dooming Viola to instant death out of sheer jealousy, but she loved him so much that she said she would most joyfully suffer death to give her master ease.

However, Olivia was far from willing to lose her husband and she called out, 'Where are you going, my Cesario?'

Viola replied, 'After the man I love more than my life.' Olivia stopped them both in their tracks by shouting that Cesario was her husband. She sent for the priest who declared that not two hours had passed since he had married Lady Olivia to this young man. Viola protested that she was not married to Olivia but no one believed her. Olivia's evidence and the words of the priest convinced Orsino that this page had robbed him of the treasure he prized above his life. Thinking that the situation was past saving, he was saying goodbye to his faithless love and the young pretender, her husband, as he called Viola, warning her never to come in his sight again, when a miracle appeared! Another Cesario came along and called Olivia as his wife. This new Cesario was Sebastian, Olivia's real husband. When their surprise at seeing two people with the same face, the same voice and the same clothes had calmed down a little, brother and sister began to question each other. Viola could hardly belive that her brother was alive and Sebastian had no idea how to account for the sister he supposed drowned being found dressed as

a young man. Viola soon admitted that she was indeed Viola and his sister under that disguise.

When all the mistakes had been cleared up, they laughed at the Lady Olivia for falling in love with a woman. Olivia thought it was a fair exchange when she found out she had married the brother instead of the sister.

Orsino's hopes were ended forever by this marriage, but his fruitless love seemed to vanish. His thoughts were fixed on his favourite, young Cesario, being changed into a woman. He looked at Viola with care and he remembered how very handsome he had always thought Cesario was. He decided that she would look very beautiful in women's clothes. Then he remembered how often she had said she loved him, which at that time seemed only the dutiful expressions of a faithful page. Now he guessed that she had meant something more, for many of her pretty sayings, which were like riddles to him, came into his mind. No sooner had he remembered all these things than he decided to make Viola his wife. He said to her — still he could not help calling her Cesario and boy — 'Boy, you have said to me a thousand times that you would never love a woman. For the faithful service you have given me and as you have called me master for so long, you shall now be your master's mistress and Orsino's true duchess.'

Olivia realized that Orsino was giving the heart which she had so ungraciously rejected to Viola and she invited them to enter her house. She offered them the assistance of the good priest who had married her to Sebastian in the morning to perform the same ceremony in the afternoon for Orsino and Viola. So the twin brother and sister were both married on the same day. The storm and shipwreck which had separated them had become the means of bringing them happiness. Viola was the wife of Orsino, the Duke of Illyria, and Sebastian the husband of the rich and noble countess, the Lady Olivia.

Romeo and Juliet

The two chief families of the city of Verona were the Capulets and the Montagues. There had been a quarrel between these families and now they hated each other so much that the enmity extended to the most distant relations, the followers and servants of both families. A servant of the house of Montague could not meet a servant of the house of Capulet, nor a member of the Capulet family encounter a Montague even by accident, without fierce words and sometimes bloodshed following. Frequent brawls from such accidental meetings disturbed the happy peace of Verona's streets.

Old Lord Capulet was giving a great supper party to which he had invited many beautiful ladies and other noble guests. All the most admired beauties of Verona were present and everyone was made welcome so long as they were not of the house of Montague. One of the guests was called Rosaline. She was loved by Romeo, the son of old Lord Montague. Romeo's friend Benvolio had persuaded him to go to the Capulet's party, in spite of the danger, so that he could compare his beloved Rosaline with the choicest beauties of Verona. Benvolio said that they would make him think his swan was a crow, in other words that Rosaline wasn't as beautiful as he claimed. Romeo had little faith in Benvolio's words but he was, nevertheless, persuaded to go. Romeo was a passionate lover, who lost sleep over his love and deserted his friends so that he could be alone thinking about Rosaline. She on the other hand had absolutely no interest in him at all and Benvolio wanted to cure his friend of this love by showing him how many other lovely girls there were. So Romeo, Benvolio and their friend Mercutio, dressed in carnival clothes and wearing masks, went to the Capulet's feast.

Old Lord Capulet welcomed them and told them that the ladies who did not suffer from corns were sure to dance with them. The old man was light-hearted and merry and told them how he had worn a mask when he was a young man and whispered stories in a pretty lady's ear.

They started dancing and Romeo was suddenly struck with the extraordinary beauty of one of the dancers. She was so lovely she seemed to him to teach the torches how to burn brightly. He said she was so much more beautiful than all the other girls that she was like a snow-white dove surrounded by a flock of crows. He was overheard praising this beautiful girl by Tybalt, Lord Capulet's nephew. He recognized Romeo's voice and being quick to anger, was furious that a Montague should hide himself behind a mask and come to laugh at them in their own house. He stormed and raged and would have struck young Romeo dead, but Lord Capulet would not let him fight, partly out of respect to his guests and partly because Romeo had behaved like a gentleman. Tybalt, forced to be patient against his will, restrained himself but swore that this vile Montague should pay dearly for his intrusion later.

When the dancing was over, Romeo looked around to see where the girl was standing. Still wearing his mask, he gently took her hand, calling it a shrine and saying that if he profaned it by touching it, he was a blushing pilgrim and would kiss it for atonement. 'Good pilgrim,' answered the girl, 'your devotion is too wordly. Saints have hands, which pilgrims may touch, but not kiss.'

'Do saints not have lips, and don't pilgrims have them too?' Romeo asked.

'Yes,' said the girl, 'lips which they must use in prayer.'

'Oh, then, my dear saint,' said Romeo, 'hear my prayer and grant it, in case I despair!' They were busy with these loving and witty words when the girl was called away to her mother. Romeo, asking who her mother was, discovered that he had been talking to young Juliet, daughter and heir to Lord Capulet. He had fallen in love with his family's enemy. This worried him but it could not stop him from loving.

Juliet was just as worried when she found that the man she had been talking to was Romeo and a Montague, for she had fallen just as suddenly in love with him as he had with her. It seemed now to her that she should love her enemy and that her feelings should settle on a person whom family considerations should make her hate.

At midnight, Romeo and his friends went home, but they soon missed him because, unable to stay away from Juliet, he climbed the wall of an orchard at the back of Juliet's house. He was standing there thinking about his new love, when Juliet appeared at the window. Her amazing beauty seemed to him to shine like the dawn and the faint light of the moon appeared to Romeo as if it were sick and pale with grief at the superior brightness of this new sun. She rested her cheek on her hand and Romeo was so much in love that he wished he were a glove on that hand so that he might touch her cheek. Juliet, thinking herself alone, sighed deeply and exclaimed, 'Oh, dear!'

Romeo was thrilled to hear her speak and said softly and unheard by Juliet, 'Oh, speak again.'

Unaware of being overheard and full of her feelings of love, Juliet called her lover's name, 'O, Romeo! Romeo!' she said, 'Why do you have to be Romeo? Leave your father and refuse your name for my sake; or if you do not want to do that, just be my love and I will no longer be a Capulet.' Romeo, encouraged by her words, would have spoken but he wanted of hearing more. Juliet continued still scolding Romeo for being Romeo and

a Montague and wishing he had some other name. She wished that he would discard that hated name and take all of her as payment for losing his name.

At this, Romeo could no longer hold himself, but joined in the conversation as if her words had been spoken to him personally and not merely to herself. He asked her to call him Love or by any other name she pleased, for he would no longer be Romeo if that name was hateful to her. Juliet, alarmed at hearing a man's voice coming from the garden, did not at first know who, under cover of night and darkness, had stumbled on her secret. When he spoke again, although they had talked only a little earlier in the evening, she immediately recognized his voice. She told him off about putting himself in such danger by climbing the orchard wall, for if any of her family found him, a Montague, there, they would kill him. Romeo said, 'There is more danger in your eyes than in twenty of their swords. If you just look at me kindly, I am protected against their enmity. I should rather my life was ended by their hate than live without your love.'

'How did you come here?' Juliet asked. 'Who directed you?'

'Love directed me,' Romeo answered. 'I am no pilot, but if you were as far away from me as that vast shore which is washed by the farthest sea, I would still find you.' Juliet blushed although the night hid her face from Romeo, when she thought about how, without meaning to, she had told Romeo of her love for him. She wished she could take back her words, but that was impossible. She wished she had behaved as she had been taught and have kept her lover at a distance. Girls were taught to frown and be difficult and to pretend they don't care so that their lovers do not think that they can be too easily won — for difficulty in getting what you want increases its value. Now there was no room for any of this. Romeo had heard her admit that she loved him from her own lips when she did not dream that he was near her. So, with complete honesty, she confirmed the truth of what he had already heard. Calling him fair Montague — love can sweeten a sour name — she asked him not to assume that her admission of love meant that she had an unworthy mind. If there were any blame, he must blame the night, which had so strangely uncovered her thoughts. She added that though her behaviour to him might not be very wise in a young girl, she would prove truer than many who pretended to be wise and well-behaved.

Romeo was just beginning to ask heaven to witness that nothing was farther from his thoughts than to suggest even a shadow of dishonour to such respectable girl, when she stopped him. She begged him not to swear, for although she delighted in his love, she thought that what happened that night was too rash, too ill-advised and too sudden. Romeo urged her to exchange promises of love. She replied that she had already given

him her promise before he asked for it, meaning when he had overheard her talking to herself. She added that she would take back what she had given then, for the pleasure of giving it all over again. She said that generosity was as huge as the sea and her love as deep.

Just then, Juliet's nurse, who had looked after her when she was a little girl and still slept in her room, called her and said it was time for her to be in bed, for it was nearly dawn. Returning briefly she said a few more words to Romeo, saying that if his love was true and he meant to marry her, she would send a messenger to him tomorrow to arrange a time for their wedding. While they were arranging this, Juliet's nurse repeatedly called her. So she went in and came back again because she didn't want Romeo to go away. He was just as unwilling to part from her, for the sweetest music to lovers is the sound of each other's voices. At last they parted, wishing each other sweet sleep and rest for that night.

The day was dawning when they parted. Romeo was too full of thoughts of Juliet to be able to sleep, so instead of going home, he set off for the nearby monastery to find Friar Laurence. The good friar was already up at his prayers, but seeing young Romeo about so early, he guessed rightly that he had not been to bed that night but had been kept awake by thoughts of love. He was right in guessing that love had kept Romeo awake but he made a wrong guess at the girl, for he thought that thoughts of Rosaline had kept him awake. When Romeo revealed his new love for Juliet and asked the friar to marry them that day, the holy man raised his eyes and hands in amazement at the sudden change in Romeo's feelings, for Romeo had told him all about Rosaline and how she ignored him. The friar said that young men's love was not true love from the heart but they were simply deluded by a pretty face. Romeo reminded him that he himself had often told him off for doting on Rosaline who did not love him in return whereas Juliet both loved him and was loved by him. The friar agreed that this sounded more like true love. He thought that if Juliet and Romeo were married, this might perhaps be the means of making up the long-standing quarrel between the Capulets and the Montagues. The good friar was a friend of both the families and had often tried to end the quarrel but had never managed to. Partly because he hoped the Montagues and Capulets would become friends and partly because he was very fond of Romeo, the old man agreed to marry the young couple.

Romeo felt that he was truly blessed. Juliet, who knew his plan from a messenger she had sent as she had promised, arrived early at Friar Laurence's cell. There, they were married and the good friar prayed that the heavens would smile on the wedding and the joining of this young Montague and young Capulet to bury the old strife and long quarrels of their families.

When the wedding was over, Juliet hurried to wait impatiently for the coming night, when Romeo had promised to meet her in the orchard where they had met the night before. The time between seemed as tedious to her as the night before some great festival seems to an impatient child, who has new party clothes that she may not put on till the morning.

About noon, the same day, Romeo's friends Benvolio and Mercutio were walking through the streets of Verona, when they met a group of Capulets led by Tybalt. It was Tybalt who wanted to fight with Romeo at old Lord Capulet's feast. Seeing Mercutio, he accused him of being Romeo's friend, the friend of a Montague. Mercutio, who was as quick-tempered as Tybalt, replied sharply. In spite of all Benvolio could say to calm the situation down, a quarrel was beginning, when Romeo himself came along. Tybalt turned from Mercutio to Romeo and called him a villain. Romeo wanted to avoid a quarrel with Tybalt more than anyone, because he was Juliet's cousin and she loved him very much. In any case, Romeo, who was wise and gentle by nature, had never thoroughly entered into the family quarrel. In fact, the name of Capulet, Juliet's name, was now a charm to calm anger rather than a word to excite fury. So he tried to reason

with Tybalt, whom he greeted politely by the name of good Capulet, as if he, though a Montague, had some secret pleasure in saying that name. Tybalt, who hated all Montagues as he hated hell, would not listen to reason but drew his sword. Meanwhile, Mercutio, who did not know why Romeo wanted peace with Tybalt and who thought he was being cowardly, provoked a quarrel with many scornful words. Tybalt and Mercutio fought each other while Romeo and Benvolio tried to part them. Tybalt thrust his sword and Mercutio fell dead. Romeo lost his temper and returned the scornful insult of 'villain' to Tybalt. They fought till Tybalt was killed by Romeo.

This deadly fight had taken place in the middle of Verona at mid-day, so a crowd quickly gathered, among it Lord Capulet and Lord Montague with their wives. Soon after the prince himself arrived. He was related to Mercutio, whom Tybalt had killed. As the peace of his principality was often disturbed by these brawls of Montagues and Capulets, he came determined to put the law in strictest force against those who offended. The prince ordered Benvolio to tell him what had happened. He did so, keeping as near to the truth as he could without harming Romeo, minimizing and excusing the part which his friend had played. Lady Capulet, who was heartbroken at the death of her nephew Tybalt, was full of feelings of revenge. She asked the prince to do strict justice upon his murderer and to pay no attention to Benvolio who was, she said, Romeo's friend and a Montague and not an impartial witness. In this way she pleaded against her new son-in-law, although she did not know that he was Juliet's husband. On the other hand, Lady Montague begged for her son's life; arguing, with some justice, that Romeo had done nothing worthy of punishment in taking the life of Tybalt, whom the law would have condemned because he had killed Mercutio. The prince, unmoved by the desperate claims of the two women, after a careful examination of the facts, pronounced his sentence. Romeo was to be sent away from Verona for ever.

Poor Juliet, who had been a wife for only a few hours, now seemed to be divorced for ever. When the news first reached her, she gave way to rage against Romeo, who had killed her dear cousin. She called him a beautiful tyrant, an angelic devil, a ravenous dove, a lamb with a wolf's nature, a snake heart hidden with a flowering face and many other contradictory names, which only showed the struggle in her mind between her love and her anger. In the end, love won and the tears which she shed for sadness that Romeo had killed her cousin turned to drops of joy that her husband whom Tybalt would have killed, lived. Then came fresh tears and they were all because of Romeo's banishment. His being sent away for ever was more terrible to her than the death of many Tybalts.

After the fight, Romeo had taken refuge in Friar Laurence's cell. It was here that he first learned of the prince's sentence, which seemed to him far more terrible than death. He felt as if there was no world outside Verona and no life out of sight of Juliet. Heaven was where Juliet lived and everywhere else was purgatory, torture, hell. The good friar wanted to comfort him but the frantic young man would not listen. Like a madman, he tore his hair and threw himself down on the ground, as he said, to be measured for his grave. He was roused by a message from Juliet, which revived him a little. Then the friar took the opportunity to tell him off for his feeble behaviour. He had killed Tybalt, but would he also kill himself and Juliet, who lived only for him. The law had been kind to him; instead of a fair sentence of death, he was only banished. He had killed Tybalt, but Tybalt would have killed him; there was a sort of satisfaction in that. Juliet was alive and had become his wife and this was his greatest reason for happiness. All these blessings, as the friar made them out to be, Romeo pushed aside like a spoiled child. Then the friar told him to beware, for those who despaired died miserable. When Romeo had calmed down, he advised him to go that night secretly to say goodbye to Juliet, and then go straight to Mantua. He should stay there till the friar found a suitable occasion to announce his marriage. This might be a joyful means of making the two families friends and he was sure that the prince would be moved to pardon him. He would return with twenty times more joy than his sadness on leaving. Romeo was convinced by the friar's wise counsels. He said goodbye and went to find Juliet, intending to stay with her that night and leave for Mantua by daybreak. The good friar promised to send him letters from time to time to let him know what was happening at home.

Romeo spent that night with his dear wife, climbing secretly up to her room from the orchard from where he had heard her admit her love for him the night before. It had been a night of unmixed joy and rapture, but the delight the lovers took in each other's company was sadly spoiled by the prospect of parting and the fatal adventures of the previous day. The unwelcome dawn seemed to come too soon and when Juliet heard the morning song of the lark, she tried to persuade herself it was the nightingale, which sings by night. It was too truly the lark and its song seemed discordant and horrible to her. Streaks of day in the east, too, certainly pointed out that it was time for the lovers to part. Romeo said goodbye to his dear wife with a heavy heart, promising to write to her from Mantua every hour of the day. When he had climbed from her window, he stood below her on the ground, in a sad and worrying state of mind, but he was forced to hurry away, for it was death for him to be found within the city of Verona after daybreak.

This was just the beginning of the tragedy of this pair of star-crossed lovers. Romeo had not been gone many days before Lord Capulet suggested that Juliet should get married. The husband he had chosen for her, not dreaming that she was married already, was Count Paris. He was a brave, young and noble man, who would have made a good husband to young Juliet, if she had never seen Romeo.

Juliet was terrified and confused by her father's suggestion. She said that she was too young, that the recent death of Tybalt had left her too unhappy to meet a husband with any pretence of joy, and that it would be unsuitable for the family of Capulets to celebrate a wedding when his funeral was hardly over. She urged every reason against the marriage but the true one, that she was married already. Lord Capulet was deaf to all her excuses and sternly ordered her to get ready to marry Paris the following Thursday.

He told her that he had found her a rich, young and noble husband, such as the proudest girl in Verona might joyfully accept, so he could not bear that she should put obstacles in the way of her own good fortune out of sheer silliness.

In desperation, Juliet went to the friendly friar for help. He always advised her when she was in distress. He asked her if she had enough strength of mind to undertake a desperate solution, and she answered that she would do anything rather than marry Paris while her own dear husband was living. He told her to go home and appear merry. She was to say that she agreed to marry Paris as her father wished. The next night, on the eve of the wedding, she must swallow the contents of a little bottle he gave her. For forty-two hours after drinking it, she would appear cold and lifeless, so that when her bridegroom came to fetch her in the morning, he would think she was dead. Then she would be carried, as was usual in that country, on an uncovered bier to be buried in the family vault. If she could be brave and agree to this terrible trial, in forty-two hours after swallowing the liquid she would be sure to awake as if from a dream. Before then, he would let her husband know their plan, so that he could come in the night and take her to Mantua. Love for Romeo and the dread of marrying Paris gave young Juliet strength to undertake this horrible adventure. She took the little bottle from the friar, promising to follow his instructions.

When she left the monastery, she met Count Paris and promised to become his bride. This was a good news to Lord Capulet and his wife. It seemed to put youth into the old man and Juliet, who had made him very annoyed by her refusal of the count, was his darling again. All the house was in a bustle preparing for the wedding. No cost was spared in preparing a celebration such as Verona had never before witnessed.

On the Wednesday night Juliet drank the potion. She was very worried in case the friar, to avoid being blamed for marrying her to Romeo, had given her poison but then he was well known as a holy man. Then she was worried that she might wake up before the time Romeo was due to come for her. She was afraid the terror of the place, a vault of the dead Capulet's bones, where Tybalt lay in his shroud, would drive her distracted.

She thought of all the stories she had heard of spirits haunting the place where their bodies were layed. Finally, her love for Romeo and her dislike of Paris returned, she desperately swallowed the potion and became unconscious.

Early in the morning Paris arrived to awaken his bride. Instead of a living Juliet, her room presented the dreary spectacle of a lifeless corpse. What death to his hopes! What confusion there was then through the whole house! Poor Paris was heartbroken over the death of his bride. The grief of old Lord and Lady Capulet was even greater. They had had only this one loving child, whom they loved and cared for, and now cruel death had snatched her from them, just as they were on the point of seeing her make a good and happy marriage. Everything that had been prepared for the wedding celebration was turned to be used for the funeral. The wedding party served for a sad burial feast, the bridal hymns were changed to miserable dirges, the lively instruments to melancholy bells, and the flowers that should have been strewn in the bride's path now served scatter on her corpse. Instead of a priest to marry her, a priest was needed to bury her and she was carried to church, not to add to the cheerful hopes of the living but to swell the dreary numbers of the dead.

Bad news always travels faster than good and the dismal story of Juliet's death reached Romeo in Mantua before the messenger sent by Friar Laurence arrived with the real details. Romeo had been unusually joyful and light-hearted. He had had a dream that he was dead (a strange dream that let a dead man think) and that Juliet came and breathed such life with kisses on his lips that he revived and was an emperor! When a messenger came from Verona, he was sure that it was to confirm some good news which his dreams had foretold. When the news turned out to be the opposite, that it was his wife who was really dead, he ordered horses to be got ready so that he could visit Verona and see his lady in her tomb that night.

As mischief is quick to enter into the thoughts of desperate men, he remembered a poor apothecary, a son of a chemist whose shop in Mantua he had recently passed. From the poverty-stricken appearance of the man, who looked as if he were starving, the wretched display of empty boxes ranged on dirty shelves in his shop and other signs of misery, he had said at the time, 'If a man were to need poison, which it is illegal to sell in Mantua, this poor wretch would sell it him.' These words now came back into his mind and he went to look for the apothecary. After pretending to have doubts and the offer of gold, the apothecary sold him a poison, which, he said, would kill him even if he had the strength of twenty men.

With this poison, he set out for Verona, to see his dear wife in her tomb, meaning to

swallow the poison and be buried by her side. He reached Verona at midnight and found the churchyard in the middle of which was the ancient tomb of the Capulets. He had brought a lantern, a spade and crowbar and was just about to break open the monument, when he was interrupted by someone calling out 'Vile Montague' and telling him to stop. It was Count Paris, who had come to Juliet's tomb to scatter flowers and to cry over the grave of the girl who should have been his bride. He did not know what an interest Romeo had in the dead but, knowing him to be a Montague and so a sworn enemy to all the Capulets, he guessed that he had come at night to do something dreadful to the dead bodies. Angrily, he told him to stop and as he recognized Romeo, a criminal, condemned by the laws of Verona to die if he were found within the city, he would have arrested him. Romeo urged Paris to leave him alone and reminded him what had happened to Tybalt, who lay buried there. He warned Paris not to provoke his anger or draw down another sin upon his head by forcing him to kill him. The count scornfully ignored his warning and tried to arrest him. Romeo fought back and Paris fell dead. Romeo with the help of his lantern looked at the dead man's face and recognized Paris. On his way from Mantua he had learned that Paris was to have married Juliet and he took the dead man by the hand as a friend in misfortune. He said that he would bury

Paris in a triumphal grave, meaning in Juliet's grave, which he now opened. There lay Juliet, unchanged by death and beautiful as ever. She lay fresh and blooming, just as she had fallen asleep when she swallowed the numbing potion. Near her lay Tybalt, and when Romeo saw him he begged pardon of his lifeless corpse. For Juliet's sake he called him cousin and said that he was about to do him a favour by putting his enemy, meaning himself, to death.

Romeo kissed Juliet goodbye and swallowed the poison which the apothecary had sold him. This poison was fatal and real, not like the potion which Juliet had swallowed, which only faked death. The effect of this potion was beginning to wear off and she about to awake.

It was now the time which the friar had promised that Juliet would wake up. Having learned that his letters, by a piece of bad luck, had never reached Romeo, he came himself, provided with a pickaxe and lantern, to rescue her from the the tomb. He was surprised to find a light already burning in the Capulet's monument and to see swords and blood and Romeo and Paris lying breathless by it.

Before he could begin to work out what happened, Juliet awoke. Seeing the friar she

remembered where she was and why, and asked for Romeo. The friar, hearing a noise, asked her to come out of that place of death and of unnatural sleep, for a greater Power than they had disturbed their plans. Frightened by the noise of people coming, he ran away. Juliet saw the cup clasped in her true love's hands and guessed that poison had caused his death. She would have drunk the dregs if any had been left and she kissed his still warm lips to see if any poison still remained upon them. Then, hearing the sound of people coming nearer she quickly unsheathed Romeo's dagger and stabbed herself. She died by her true Romeo's side.

By this time, the night watchmen had reached the place. Count Paris's page who had witnessed the fight between his master and Romeo, had given the alarm. This had spread among the people, who went up and down the streets of Verona confusedly shouting. 'Paris! Romeo! Juliet!' The uproar brought Lord Montague and Lord Capulet and the prince out of their beds to inquire into the cause of the disturbance. The friar had been arrested by some of the watchmen, as he came out of the churchyard, trembling, sighing and crying in a suspicious manner. A great crowd gathered at the Capulet's monument and the prince ordered the friar to tell what he knew of these strange and disastrous accidents.

Here, in the presence of the old Lords Montague and Capulet, he faithfully told the story of their children's fatal love and the part he took in helping their marriage in the hope that it would end the long quarrels between their families. He spoke of how Romeo — there dead — was husband to Juliet, and Juliet — there dead — was Romeo's faithful wife and how, before he could find an opportunity to announce their marriage, another marriage was planned for Juliet. He explained how she, to avoid the crime of a second marriage, swallowed the sleeping potion, as he advised, and how everyone had thought she was dead. He said how he had written to Romeo to come and take her to Mantua when the potion wore off and how the letters had never reached him. He knew more. He himself had come to rescue Juliet from that place of death and had found Count Paris and Romeo dead. The rest of the story was supplied by the page who had seen Paris and Romeo fight, and by the servant who came with Romeo from Verona. Romeo had given him letters to be delivered to his father in the event of his death, which admitted his marriage to Juliet, asked forgiveness of his parents, told of the buying of the poison from the poor apothecary and his plan in coming to the monument to die and lay beside Juliet. All these details agreed and cleared the friar from any charge of causing deaths other than as the unexpected and unintended result of his own well-meant attempts to help Juliet.

The prince, turning to the old Lords, Montague and Capulet, rebuked them for their brutal and stupid enmity. He pointed out what a suffering Heaven had laid upon such offences that it had punished their unnatural hate through the love of their children. These old rivals, no longer enemies, agreed to bury their long quarrel in their children's graves. Lord Capulet asked Lord Montague to give him his hand, calling him brother, as if admitting the joining of their families by the marriage of the young Capulet and Montague. Lord Montague said that he would build a statue of pure gold so that while Verona still existed, no one should be more highly prized than the true and faithful Juliet. Lord Capulet, in return, said that he would build another statue — this one to Romeo. Now when it was far too late, these two poor old lords tried to outdo each other in acts of friendship and kindness. So deadly had been their rage and enmity in the past, that nothing except the deaths of their beloved children could remove the rooted hates and jealousies of the noble families.

Hamlet, Prince of Denmark

Less than two months after the King's death, his widow, Queen Gertrude, married her brother-in-law, Claudius. At the time people thought her action was unfeeling or worse, for Claudius was not at all like the dead king, either in his appearance or his character. He was unattractive and unworthy in every way and some people suspected that he had secretly killed his brother, the late king, with a view to marry his widow and to ascend the throne of Denmark, which rightfully belonged to Hamlet, the son of the buried king.

No one was more distressed by the queen's behaviour than this young prince, who loved and respected the memory of his dead father almost to idolatry. His own sense of honour and proper behaviour made his mother's remarriage seem even more unworthy. Between grief for his father's death and shame for his mother's marriage, this young prince sank into a deep sadness and lost all his cheerfulness and all his good looks. He lost all his usual interest in books and the activities and sports that young men normally enjoy were no longer a pleasure. He grew tired of the world, which seemed to him like an unweeded garden, where all the flowers were choked and nothing but weeds could thrive.

It was not that the throne, his lawful inheritance, had been stolen from him which upset him so much, although it was a bitter wound and a sore indignity to a young and high-minded prince, it was that his mother had shown herself so forgetful of his father's memory. He had been such a splendid father and a loving and gentle husband, too! She had always appeared to be a loving and obedient a wife to him, yet within two months she had married again. What was more, she had married his uncle, her dead husband's brother, which was in itself improper and against the law because they were so closely related, but which was made much worse by the indecent hurry and the unkingly character of the man whom she had chosen to share the throne. It was this, more than the loss of ten kingdoms, that dashed the spirits and brought a cloud over the mind of this honourable young prince.

Neither his mother Gertrude nor the king could do anything to cheer him up. He still appeared in court in a suit of deep black, as mourning for his father's death. He never wore any other colour, even on his mother's wedding day, nor could he be brought to join in any of the festivities or celebrations.

What troubled him most was an uncertainty about the way his father had died. Claudius claimed that a snake had bitten him, but young Hamlet had shrewd suspicions that Claudius himself was the snake; in other words, that he had murdered him for his crown. The snake that had bitten his father now sat on his throne. Doubts and worries continually weighed on his mind. How far he was right in his guess and what ought he think of his mother — how much did she know of this murder and had she agreed to it?

A rumour had reached Hamlet that a ghost, which looked exactly like the dead king, had been seen by the soldiers on watch on two or three nights in succession. The figure always wore the same suit of armour, which the dead king was known to have worn. Everyone who had seen it, including Hamlet's friend Horatio, agreed about the time and way it appeared. It came just as the clock struck twelve. It looked pale, with a sad rather than angry face. Its beard was grey, as they had seen it in his lifetime. It didn't answer when they spoke to it, yet once they thought it lifted up its head and looked as if it were about to speak, but just at that moment the cock crowed and it hurriedly vanished from their sight.

The young prince was amazed at their story and as all the details agreed, he thought it must be true. He decided that it was his father's ghost they had seen and determined to watch with the soldiers that night so that he might have a chance of seeing it. He reckoned that a ghost would not appear without good reason and that it had something to say. He thought that although it had been silent before, it would speak to him. He waited impatiently for the night.

When the night came, he went with Horatio and Marcellus, one of the guard, to the platform where this ghost usually appeared. It was a cold night and the air was unusually raw. Hamlet, Horatio and their companion began chatting about the coldness of the night, when Horatio suddenly announced that the ghost was coming.

The sight of his father's ghost struck Hamlet with surprise and fear. At first he called upon the angels and heavenly ministers to defend them, for he did not know whether it was a good or a bad spirit and whether it came to do good or evil. He gradually gained courage and his ghostly father looked at him so piteously as if he wanted to talk to him. In every respect he looked so like he did when he was alive, that Hamlet could not help speaking to him. He called him by his name, 'Hamlet, King, Father!' and asked him why he had left his grave, where he had been quietly laid to rest, to come and visit the earth again. He asked if there was anything they could do to give peace to his spirit. The ghost

beckoned Hamlet towards a quieter place, where they could be alone. Horatio and Marcellus tried to persuade Hamlet not to go with the ghost in case it turned out to be an evil spirit that would tempt him into the sea or to the top of some dreadful cliff, where it might turn into something horrible and drive him mad. Neither their advice nor their pleas could alter Hamlet's determination. He cared too little about life to fear losing it and, as for his soul, he said, what could a ghost do to that as it was immortal as itself? He felt brave as a lion and bursting free from the friends who tried to hold him back, he followed wherever the ghost led him.

When they were alone together, the ghost broke its silence and told Hamlet that he was the ghost of his father. He had been cruelly murdered by his own brother Claudius, just as Hamlet had suspected, in the hope of succeeding to the crown. He had been asleep in the garden, taking his usual afternoon nap, when his brother crept up and poured the poisonous juice of henbane into his ears. This plant is so poisonous that it spreads through all the veins of the body like fire, baking the blood and spreading a crust all over the skin. He made Hamlet promise that if he ever loved his father, he would revenge his foul murder. The ghost complained bitterly that Hamlet's mother should sink so low as to prove false to the love of her first husband and to marry his murderer. Finally he warned Hamlet that whatever revenge he took against his wicked uncle, he must not harm his mother, but should leave her to Heaven and to the stings and thorns of her own conscience. Hamlet promised to follow the ghost's instructions and the ghost vanished.

When Hamlet was left alone, he made a solemn promise that everything he had in his memory, either learned from books or just from looking, should be instantly forgotten and nothing stay in his brain except the memory what the ghost had told him and asked him to do. Hamlet told no one about what the ghost had said except his best friend Horatio. He made both Horatio and Marcellus promise the strictest secrecy about what they had seen that night.

The terror which the sight of the ghost had left upon Hamlet's senses, especially as he was already weak and dispirited, almost unhinged his mind and drove him mad. He was worried that this might continue and set his uncle on his guard. Hamlet did not want Claudius to suspect that he was planning anything against him or that he really knew more about his father's death than he said. He made a strange decision to pretend that he really and truly was mad. This would make his uncle think that he was incapable of any serious project and would also disguise his real worries.

From this time, Hamlet started to dress strangely and to speak and behave in an odd way. He pretended madness so well that the king and the queen were both deceived. They did not think his grief for his father's death was enough to produce such a problem — for they did not know of the appearance of the ghost — so they assumed that he had fallen in love. They also thought they had found out the name of the girl he was in love with.

Before all this happened Hamlet had been very fond of a pretty girl called Ophelia. She was a daughter of Polonius, the king's chief counsellor in affairs of state. He had sent her letters, rings and other tokens of his affection for her and spoken to her of love. She had believed his promises and requests. The sadness caused by his father's death and mother's remarriage had made him neglect her, and once he had thought of the idea of pretending to be mad, he began to treat her with unkindness and a sort of rudeness. She, rather than complain to him of being false to her, persuaded herself that it was only his illness and not real unkindness that had made him less thoughtful of her than before.

Though the rough business of revenge which Hamlet had in hand did not go very well with the playful state of courtship, and although he now thought of love as wasted time, soft thoughts of Ophelia would now and then come into his mind. Once, when he thought that his treatment of this gentle lady had been unreasonably harsh, he wrote her a letter full of wild and elaborate words that seemed to express his supposed madness, but mixed with some gentle touches of affection, which showed Ophelia that a deep love for her still lay at the bottom of his heart. He asked her to doubt that the stars were fiery, to doubt that the sun moved, to believe that truth was a liar, but never to doubt that he loved. Ophelia dutifully showed this letter to her father and the old man thought himself bound to tell the king and the queen about it. From that time, they supposed that the true cause of Hamlet's madness was love. The queen hoped that the beauty of Ophelia was the cause of his wildness so that her goodness might restore him to his usual way again.

However, Hamlet's problems lay deeper than she supposed and than could be cured in this way. His father's ghost still haunted his imagination and the sacred order to revenge his murder gave Hamlet no rest. Every hour of delay seemed to him a sin and disobedience of his father's commands. Yet killing the king, who was always surrounded by his guards, was no easy matter. Even if he solved this difficulty, his mother, the queen, was generally with the king and this put a stop to his plans. The fact that the false king was his mother's husband filled him with pity and further blunted the edge of his purpose. The idea of putting any fellow creature to death was also hateful and terrible to someone as naturally gentle as Hamlet. His very sadness and misery made it hard for

him to make up his mind to act. Moreover, he was also unsure whether the ghost he had seen was really his father or whether it might have been the devil, who, he had heard, has power to look like anyone he pleases. He might have made himself look like Hamlet's father only to take advantage of his weakness and misery, to drive him to so desperate an act as murder. He decided that he must have more proof than a vision or a ghost, which might simply be a delusion.

While he was in this uncertain frame of mind, a troop of travelling actors arrived at the court. Hamlet used to enjoy their performances, particularly when one of them made a tragic speech describing the death of old Priam, King of Troy, and the grief of Hecuba, his queen. Hamlet welcomed his old friends the actors and remembering how he enjoyed that speech, asked the player to repeat it. He did so in such a lively way, setting forth the cruel murder of the feeble old king, the destruction of his people and city by fire, and the mad grief of the old queen, running barefoot up and down the palace, with a poor rag upon that head where a crown had been and only a blanket wrapped around her where she had worn a royal robe, that it drew tears from everyone listening. Even the actor himself spoke in a broken voice and cried real tears.

This made Hamlet think. If an actor could work himself up to such strong feelings by a mere fictitious speech, to cry for someone he had never seen — for Hecuba who had been dead for hundreds of years — how dull he was, when he had a real motive and reason for strong feelings. His dear father had been murdered, and yet he seemed to care so little that his revenge had been forgotten. While he was thinking about actors and acting and the powerful effect a good play has upon the audience, he remembered the story of a murderer, who, seeing a murder on the stage, was so upset that, on the spot, he admitted the crime which he had committed. He decided that these actors should act out something like the murder of his father before his uncle. He would watch his uncle closely to see what effect it had upon him and decide from his looks if he were the murderer or not. He ordered a play to be prepared and invited the king and queen to come and see it.

The story of the play was of a duke's murder committed in Vienna. The duke's name was Gonzago and his wife was called Baptista. The play showed how Lucianus, a near relation to the duke, poisoned him in his garden so that he could steal his estate and how the murderer shortly afterwards gained the love of Gonzago's wife.

The king, who did not know the trap set for him, the queen and the whole court came to watch the play. Hamlet sat near the king so that he could watch him. The play began with a conversation between Gonzago and his wife. She made many promises of

love, saying she would never marry a second husband if she outlived Gonzago. She wished that she would be cursed if she ever remarried, adding that no woman ever did so except wicked women who kill their first husbands. Hamlet watched the king, his uncle, change colour at this. When Lucianus, according to the story, came to poison Gonzago who was sleeping in the garden, the strong similarity to his own wicked act upset Claudius so much that he was unable to sit out the rest of the play. He called for candles to be taken to his room, and pretending or partly feeling a sudden sickness, he abruptly left the theatre. When the king left, the play ended. Now Hamlet had seen enough to be satisfied that the words of the ghost were true. In a burst of happiness, like that which comes over a man who suddenly has some great doubt removed, he swore to Horatio that he would take the ghost's word for a thousand pounds. Before he could decide how to go about his revenge, now that he was sure that his uncle was his father's murderer, the queen sent for him to come and talk to her in private.

It was the king's wish that the queen should speak to Hamlet about how much he had annoyed them both. The king wanted to know everything mother and son said to each other. However, he thought that Gertrude might not tell him everything because she was Hamlet's mother and did not want him to get into trouble. So Polonius, the old counsellor of state, was ordered to hide himself behind a curtain in the queen's room where he could listen to everything without being seen. This plan suited Polonius, who loved to learn about things in an indirect and cunning way.

Hamlet came in and his mother began to tell him off about his actions and behaviour. She told him that he had offended his father, meaning the king, his uncle, whom, because he had married her, she called Hamlet's father. Hamlet was furious that she should give so dear and honoured a name as father seemed to a wretch and the murderer of his true father, and replied sharply, 'Mother, you have much offended my father.' The queen said that was a meaningless answer. 'As good as the question deserved,' Hamlet said. The queen asked him if he had forgotten to whom he was speaking. 'Sadly no!' replied Hamlet, 'I wish I could forget. You are the queen, your husband's brother's wife, and you are my mother. I wish you were not what you are.'

'Know, then,' said the queen, 'if you show me so little respect, I will get others with more authority to speak to you.' She was going to send the king or Polonius to him.

Hamlet, now that he had her alone, would not let her go till he had tried to see if his

words could not make her realize the wickedness of her life. Taking her by the wrist, he held her tightly and made her sit down. She, frightened by his seriousness and afraid he would hurt her in his madness, cried out. A voice was heard from behind the curtain, 'Help, help the queen!' Hamlet, thinking that the king himself was hiding there, drew his sword and stabbed at the place where the voice came from as he would stabbed at a rat. When the voice stopped, he assumed the person was dead. When he dragged the body out, it was not the king but Polonius, the officious old counsellor, who had hidden himself as a spy behind the curtain.

'O no!' exclaimed the queen, 'what a rash and bloody thing you have done!'

'A bloody thing, mother,' Hamlet replied, 'but not so bad as you, who killed a king and married his brother.' Hamlet had gone too far to stop now. He was in the mood to speak plainly to his mother and he did so. He pointed out to the queen the dreadfulness of her offence in forgetting the dead king, his father, so quickly that in no time at all she married his brother and his murderer. To do this after the promises she had made to her first husband was enough to make all women's promises suspect, all goodness to be counted pretence, wedding vows to be less than gamblers' oaths, and religion to be a mockery and a mere form of words. He said she had done such a dreadful thing that the heavens blushed at it and the earth was sick of her because of it. He showed her two pictures, one of the dead king, her first husband, and the other of the present king, her second husband. He told her to take notice of the difference. What grace shone from his father's face and how like a god he looked! He had had the curls of Apollo, the forehead of Jupiter, the eye of Mars and a figure like Mercury. This man, he said, had been her husband. Then he showed her her present husband. How like a blight or a mildew he looked, for so he had blasted his wholesome brother. The queen was deeply ashamed that he should turn her eyes inward upon her soul, which she now saw was black and deformed. He asked her how she could continue to live with this man and be a wife to the murderer of her first husband, who had stolen the crown like a thief. As he spoke, the ghost of his father entered the room. Hamlet, in great terror, asked what it wanted and the ghost replied that it came to remind him of the revenge he had promised and seemed to have forgotten. The ghost told him to speak more sweetly to his mother, for the grief and terror would kill her. Then it vanished but had been seen by no one except Hamlet. He could not make his mother see it either by pointing to where it stood or by any description. She was terribly frightened all this while to hear him talking, as it seemed to her, with nothing and she blamed it on the disturbance of his mind. Hamlet begged her not to flatter her wicked soul by thinking it was his madness and not her own offences which had brought his father's spirit to the earth again. He made her feel his pulse to see how gently it beat, not like a madman's. Then he begged her with tears to admit her faults to Heaven and to avoid the king's company in future. When she showed herself a proper mother to him by respecting his father's memory he would ask a blessing of her as a son. She promised to do as he said and their conversation ended.

Now Hamlet had time to consider who it was that he had killed. When he realized that it was Polonius, the father of Lady Ophelia, whom he so dearly loved, he cried for what he had done.

The unfortunate death of Polonius gave the king an excuse for sending Hamlet out of the kingdom. He would willingly have put him to death, fearing him as dangerous, but he dreaded the people, who loved Hamlet, and the queen, who doted her son. Under the pretence of providing for Hamlet's safety so he could avoid being punished for Polonius' death, Claudius arranged for him to be taken on board a ship bound for England. He was put in the care of two courtiers, who also carried letters to the English court. In these letters, Claudius invented a special reason why Hamlet should be put to death as soon as he landed on English ground. Hamlet, suspecting some treachery, secretly got at the letters in the night. Skilfully, he removed his own name and put in the names of the two courtiers who were in charge of him. He sealed up the letters and put them in their place again.

Soon afterwards, the ship was attacked by pirates. In the course of the fighting, Hamlet, wanting to show his bravery, boarded the enemy's ship. Meanwhile, his own ship in a cowardly manner sailed away, leaving him to his fate. The two courtiers made their way to England, carrying the letters, which Hamlet had altered, to their own deserved destruction.

The pirates showed themselves to be gentle enemies. Knowing whom they had as prisoner and in the hope that the prince would do them a good turn at court in return for any favour they showed him, they put Hamlet ashore at the nearest port in Denmark. Hamlet wrote to the king, informing him of the strange chance that had brought him back to his own country and saying that he would return home the next day.

When he got home, the first thing he saw was the sad sight of the funeral of the young and beautiful Ophelia. The poor girl's wits had begun to turn on her poor father's death. That he should die a violent death and at the hands of the prince she loved so affected this delicate girl that she soon grew quite mad. She would go about giving flowers to the ladies of the court, saying that they were for her father's burial. She sang songs about love and about death, and some with no meaning at all, as if she had no memory

of what happened to her. There was a willow which overgrew a brook. Ophelia came there one day with garlands of flowers that she had been making. They were mixed up from daisies and nettles, flowers and weeds. Clambering up to hang her garland upon the willow, Ophelia stepped on a branch that broke and she, her garland and all that she had gathered, fell into the water. Her clothes kept her floating for a while, during which she chanted scraps of old tunes, as if she did not understand her danger or as if she were some kind of water creature. It was not long before her clothes, heavy with water, pulled her down to a muddy and miserable death. Her brother Laertes arranged her funeral and the king, queen and whole court were attending it when Hamlet arrived.

He did not know what was going on, but stood to one side, not wanting to interrupt the ceremony. He saw the flowers scattered upon her grave, as was the custom when young girls died. The queen herself scattered flowers and as she did so, she said, 'Sweets to the sweet! I planned to decorate your bridal bed, sweet girl, not to throw flowers on

your grave. You should have been my Hamlet's wife.' He heard her brother wish that violets might spring from her grave and saw him leap into it frantic with grief. Laertes begged the attendants to pile mountains of earth upon him so that he might be buried with her. Hamlet's love for Ophelia came back to him and he could not bear her brother showing so much grief, for he thought that he loved her more than forty thousand brothers. Then, showing himself, he leaped into the grave with Laertes, as frantic or more frantic than he. Laertes, recognizing Hamlet, who had been the cause of his father's and his sister's death, began to fight him. Hamlet excused his hasty act in throwing himself into the grave as if to challenge Laertes, but he said he could not bear that anyone should seem more heartbroken than he. For the time, these two noble young men seemed friends again.

However, out of Laertes' grief and anger over the deaths of his father and Ophelia, Hamlet's wicked uncle planned his nephew's death. He persuaded Laertes, under a pretence of peace and friendship, to challenge Hamlet to a friendly fencing match. Hamlet accepted, and a day was agreed for the match. All the court had come to watch and many people had placed bets, as both Hamlet and Laertes were known to be excellent fencers. However, guided by the king, Laertes had prepared a poisoned sword. Hamlet, taking up the foils, chose one, not suspecting Laertes' treachery or bothering to examine Laertes' weapon. Instead of a blunt foil, which the rules of fencing require, Laertes had one with a point. At first, Laertes just played with Hamlet, letting him gain some points. The lying king made a lot of fuss about Hamlet's hits, drinking to his success and placing heavy bets. After a few passes, Laertes made a deadly thrust at Hamlet with his poisoned sword and made a fatal hit. Hamlet, annoyed, but unaware of the whole of the treachery, picked up Laertes' sword in the scuffle. With a thrust he repaid Laertes, who was justly caught by his own trick. At this moment the queen shrieked that she had been poisoned. She had accidentally drunk from a glass which the king had

prepared for Hamlet in case the fencing made him thirsty. The treacherous king had mixed a deadly poison in the drink to make sure of Hamlet if Laertes had failed. He had forgotten to warn the queen about the glass and she drank from it. She died immediately, exclaiming with her last breath that she had been poisoned.

Hamlet ordered the doors to be locked while he found out who was the traitor. Laertes told him to look no farther, for he was the traitor. Feeling his life slipping away, he told Hamlet of the poisoned point and said that Hamlet had no more than half an hour to live, for no medicine could cure him. He begged forgiveness of Hamlet and he died, his last words accusing the king of being the one who planned all this wrong doing. Hamlet knew he was dying but, as there was still some poison left upon the sword, he suddenly turned upon his false uncle and thrust the point of it into his heart. So he carried out the promise he had made to his father's ghost and revenged his foul murder. Hamlet, feeling himself grow weaker, turned to his dear friend Horatio, who had seen this fatal tragedy. With his dying breath he asked him to live on to tell his story to the world, for Horatio had looked as if he intended to kill himself to accompany the prince in death. Horatio promised that he would make a true report, as someone who knew everything that had happened. So the noble heart of Hamlet stopped beating and Horatio and the courtiers, with many tears, commended the spirit of their sweet prince to the guardianship of angels. Hamlet was a loving and a gentle prince, much loved for his many fine and royal qualities. If he had lived, he would, no doubt, have proved to be a great king of Denmark.

Othello

Brabantio, a rich senator of Venice, had a beautiful daughter called Desdemona. Many young men wanted to marry her both because of her goodness and her rich expectations. She was not interested in any of them, for she thought the mind was more important than good looks. Instead she had fallen in love with Othello, a Moor, whom her father loved immensely and often invited to his house. Not only was Othello black and Desdemona was white, he was also much older. He might have seemed an unsuitable choice to the people of the time but he had many excellent qualities that fitted him to be the husband of the greatest lady. He was a soldier and a brave one, too. In the terrible wars against the Turks, Othello had risen to the rank of general in the Venetian army and was respected and trusted by the state.

He had been a traveller and Desdemona loved to hear him tell the stories of his adventures. He told her of the battles, sieges and encounters he had been through, the dangers he had been exposed to by land and by water, his hair-breadth escapes, how he had been taken prisoner by the enemy and sold into slavery and how he escaped. He also described the strange things he had seen in foreign countries, the vast deserts and romantic caverns, the quarries, the rocks and mountains with their heads in the clouds, and the savage people he had met, the cannibals who are maneaters and a race of people whose heads are said to grow beneath their shoulders. These traveller's tales would so delight Desdemona that if she were called away at any time by household affairs, she would do whatever she had to do as fast as possible and return to hear more stories. Once she told him how she longed for him tell her the whole story of his life of which she had heard so much but only in parts. He agreed and caused her to cry many a tear over some sad event when he was young.

When his story was over, she sighed and said that it was all very strange, and pitiful, wondrously pitiful. She wished, she said, she had not heard it, yet she wished that Heaven had made her such a man. Then she thanked him and told him if he had a friend who loved her, he had only to teach him how to tell his story and that would win her. This hint, together with her bewitching prettiness persuaded Othello to speak more openly of his love. In this golden opportunity, he gained her agreement to marry him secretly.

Neither Othello's colour nor his fortune were such that Brabantio was likely to ac-

cept him for a son-in-law. He had left his daughter free but he expected that, like other noble Venetian ladies, she would choose a Venetian husband of senatorial rank. In this he was mistaken. Desdemona loved Othello. In fact she loved him so much that his very colour, which to other Venetian ladies of that time would have been unacceptable, seemed much better to her than all the white skins and clear complexions of the young Venetian nobles who wanted to marry her.

Their marriage — although privately carried out — could not be kept a secret for long and soon came to the ears of old Brabantio. He went to the solemn council of the senate and accused Othello of using spells and witchcraft to win Desdemona's love and persuade her to marry him without the agreement of her father and against the obligations of hospitality.

At this time news arrived that the Turks had fitted out a fleet of warships, which was sailing to the island of Cyprus, to regain the possession of the island from the Venetians. In this emergency, the state turned to Othello, who alone was thought good enough to conduct the defence of Cyprus against the Turks. So Othello was called before the senate both as a candidate for great state employment and as a culprit charged with offences of witchcraft.

Brabantio's age and dignity ensured a most patient hearing from that grave assembly but he was so angry that he could not speak clearly and just made more accusations instead of producing proof of Othello's wrongdoing. When Othello was called upon for his defence, he had only to tell a plain tale of the course of his love. He did so with such simplicity — the evidence of truth — that the duke, who sat as chief judge, could not help saying that a tale so told would have won his daughter too. The spells and magic Othello had used plainly appeared to have been no more than the honest arts of men in love and the only witchcraft he had used was a good tale to win a lady's attention.

His statement was confirmed by Lady Desdemona herself, who appeared in court. She admitted that she had a duty to her father for her life and her education, but demanded his permission to admit an even higher duty to her lord and husband. This, she pointed out, was exactly as her mother had done in preferring her husband, Brabantio, above *her* father.

The old senator, unable to maintain his case, called Othello to him with many expressions of sorrow. He had no choice but to recognize his daughter's marriage, but if he had been free to withhold her, he would have done so with all his heart. Brabantio added that he was glad that he had no more children for this behaviour of Desdemona's would have taught him to be a tyrant.

Othello was so used to the hardships of a soldier's life that he readily undertook the management of the wars in Cyprus. Desdemona, preferring the honour of her lord before those idle delights with which newly-married people usually waste their time, cheerfully agreed to his going.

No sooner had Othello and his lady landed in Cyprus, than news arrived that a terrible storm had scattered the Turkish fleet and so the island was secure from attack. Among all the general's friends, no one was closer to Othello than Michael Cassio. He was a young soldier from Florence and his good humour and charm made him a favourite among women. He was handsome and well-spoken and just the sort of person to arouse the jealousy of an older man who married a young and beautiful wife, but Othello was free from jealousy as he was noble and as incapable of suspicion as of doing a bad action. Cassio had helped him in his love affair with Desdemona and acted as

a sort of go-between in his suit. Othello knew that he himself was not very good at romantic conversations and sweet talk, so would often send Cassio to speak for him. So it was no wonder that next to Othello himself, the gentle Desdemona loved and trusted Cassio. Nor had the marriage of this couple made any difference in their behaviour to him. He often visited their house and Othello enjoyed his free and gossipy talk as a change from his own seriousness. Desdemona and Cassio would talk and laugh together, as in the days when he went to speak for his friend.

Othello had recently promoted Cassio to be lieutenant, a position of trust and responsibility. This promotion deeply offended Iago, an older officer, who thought he had a better claim than Cassio. He often mocked Cassio, as a man fit only for the company of women and a soldier who knew no more of the skills of war, or how to array an army for battle than a girl. Iago hated Cassio and he hated Othello, too, for favouring Cassio. He also wondered, though not very seriously, whether Othello was too fond of his wife Emilia. Iago planned a horrid scheme of revenge, involving Cassio, Othello and Desdemona in the same disaster.

Iago was artful and had studied human nature deeply, so that he knew that of all the torments which afflict men's minds, the pains of jealousy were the worst. If he could succeed in making Othello jealous of Cassio, he thought it would be an exquisite revenge and might end in the death of Cassio or Othello, or of both.

The arrival of the general and Desdemona in Cyprus, together with the news of the scattered enemy fleet, created a holiday mood on the island. Everybody gave themselves up to feasting and making merry. Wine flowed in abundance and everyone drank a toast to the newly-weds.

Cassio was in charge of the guard that night, with instructions from Othello not to let the soldiers drink too much. He didn't want any fights breaking out to frighten the inhabitants or disgust them with the newly landed forces. That night, Iago began his deep-laid plans of mischief. Pretending loyalty and love to the general, he encouraged Cassio to drink rather too much wine, a great fault in an officer upon guard. For a time Cassio resisted, but he could not hold out against the apparently honest generosity of Iago and swallowed glass after glass. Iago plied him with drink and encouraging songs, Cassio's tongue ran over in praise of the Lady Desdemona. He toasted her again and again and said that she was a really lovely lady. Finally his brains were completely befuddled with drink and, as a result of some silly insult from a man, Iago had encouraged, swords were drawn. Montano, a good officer, interfered to calm the quarrel and was wounded in the scuffle. The riot now began to spread. Iago, who had started everything off, was the first in spreading the alarm. He rang the castle bell as if some dangerous mutiny instead of a slight drunken quarrel had arisen. The alarm-bell ringing woke Othello, who, dressing in a hurry and coming to the scene of action, asked Cassio what had happened. Cassio had now come to himself, the effect of the wine having worn off somewhat, but he was far too ashamed to reply. Iago pretended to be very unwilling to accuse Cassio, but allowed the story to be forced from him by Othello, who insisted on knowing the truth. He told the whole story, leaving out his own share in it, which Cassio was too far gone to remember. He described things in such a way that although he seemed to make Cassio's offence less, he actually made it appear greater than it was. The result was that Othello, who was a strict observer of discipline, took away Cassio's place of lieutenant from him.

So the first stage of Iago's plan succeeded completely. He had now made his hated rival unpopular and pushed him out of his place. Further use was still to be made of the adventure of this disastrous night.

Cassio, whom this misfortune had entirely sobered, now told his friend Iago how sorry he was he should have been such a fool as to behave like an animal. He had ruined his career, for how could he ask the general for this place again? He would tell him he was a drunkard. He hated himself. Iago, pretending to make light of it, said that he or any man living might get drunk sometimes. He should now make the best of a bad bargain. The general's wife could do anything with Othello so he would be advised to apply to the Lady Desdemona to speak on his behalf. She was a kind and helpful lady and would readily agree to help Cassio to gain the general's favour again. This would have been good advice if Iago had not given it for wicked purposes.

Cassio did as Iago advised him and asked Desdemona for help. She promised Cassio that she would speak to her lord on his behalf and rather die than give up his cause. She immediately set about doing this in such a serious and pretty manner that Othello, who was still furious with Cassio, could not put her off. He said that it was too soon to pardon him, but she would not give up and insisted that it should be the next night, or the morning after, or the next morning after that at the latest. Then she told Othello how sorry and humbled poor Cassio was and said that his offence did not deserve such sharp punishment. When Othello still hung back, she said, 'What! My lord, that I should have so much to do to plead for Cassio — Michael Cassio, whom you sent to speak for you, and who, when I have complained of you, has taken your part! I think this is a very little thing to ask of you. When I really mean to test your love, I shall ask something much more important.' Othello could not refuse her and only asked that Desdemona would

leave the time to him. He then promised to receive Michael Cassio back into favour.

Just before this, Othello and Iago had entered the room where Cassio had been ask-ing Desdemona for her help. He left by the opposite door just as Othello and Iago came in. Iago, who was full of cunning, said in a low voice, as if to himself, 'I do not like that.' Othello took no great notice of what he said — indeed, the conversation with Desdem-ona which followed immediately put it out of his head — but he remembered it after-wards. When Desdemona had gone, Iago casually asked Othello whether Michael Cas-sio knew of his love for Desdemona before he married her. The general answered that he did and added that he had acted as a go-between very often. Iago frowned, as if he had got fresh light on some terrible matter, and cried, 'Indeed!' Othello remembered the words Iago had let fall when they had entered the room and seen Cassio with Des-demona. He began to think that there was some meaning in all this, for he believed Iago to be a fair man and full of affection and honesty. What would be tricks in a bad person, seemed in him to be the natural workings of an honest mind, big with something too serious to speak of. Othello asked Iago to say what he knew and to put his worst thoughts into words.

'Supposing,' said Iago, 'some very vile thoughts have intruded into my mind?' Then

Iago went on to say what a pity it would be if any trouble should arise for Othello as a result of his not seeing things clearly. It would not be for Othello's peace to know his thoughts and people's good names should not be taken away on slight suspicions. Othello's curiosity was aroused almost to distraction with these hints and stray words. Then Iago, as if out of true concern for Othello's peace of mind, warned him to beware of jealousy. Iago was very cunning in the way he aroused suspicions in the unguarded Othello by the very caution which he pretended to give him against suspicion.

'I know,' said Othello, 'that my wife is pretty, loves company and feasting, likes to chat, sings, plays and dances well, but in a good woman these are good qualities. I must have proof before I think her dishonest.'

Then Iago, as if glad that Othello was slow to believe anything wrong about his lady, frankly declared that he had no proof. He suggested that Othello should watch her behaviour well when she was with Cassio. Othello should not be jealous nor too secure either, for, Iago added, he knew the nature of Italian ladies, his countrywomen, better than Othello could do. In Venice the wives let Heaven see many pranks they dared not show their husbands. Then he shyly mentioned that Desdemona had deceived her father in marrying Othello and had been so secretive that the poor old man thought that witchcraft had been used. Othello was disturbed by this argument for if she had deceived her father, she might deceive her husband.

Iago begged pardon for having upset him but Othello, pretending he didn't care while he was really shaken with inward grief at Iago's words, asked him to go on. With many apologies, as if unwilling to produce anything against Cassio, whom he called his friend, Iago came to the point. He reminded Othello that Desdemona had refused many suitable young white Italians and had married him, which was unusual and proved to be headstrong. When her better judgement returned, it was likely that she would start to compare Othello with the fine forms and clear white complexions of the young Italians, her countrymen. He finished up by advising Othello to put off his pardoning of Cassio a little longer, and in the meantime, to note how strongly Desdemona spoke in his behalf.

The discussion ended with Iago's begging Othello to assume that his wife was innocent, until he had more decisive proof. Othello promised to be patient, but from that moment, he never had peace of mind again. Not all the sleeping potions in the world could ever again make him sleep peacefully. His occupation sickened him. He no longer took pleasure in being a general. His heart, that used to be roused at the sight of troops, banners and battle array, and that would stir at the sound of a drum, or a trumpet, or a neighing war-horse, seemed to have lost all pride and ambition. Sometimes he thought his wife was honest and at others he thought she wasn't. Then he would wish that he had never known of it. If he had not known that she loved Cassio, it could not have hurt him. Torn apart by these distracting thoughts, he once seized Iago by the throat and demanded proof of Desdemona's guilt or threatened with instant death for lying. Iago, pretending to be upset that he was not believed, asked Othello if he had not sometimes seen a handkerchief spotted with strawberries in his wife's hand. Othello answered that he had given it to her and that it was his first gift.

'That very handkerchief,' said Iago, 'Michael Cassio wiped his face with today.'

'If it is as you say,' said Othello, 'I will not rest till I am revenged. First, for a sign of your loyalty, I expect Cassio to be put to death within three days. As for that fair devil, my wife, I will think of some fast means of death for her.' To jealous people small unimportant things can seem like strong proof.

A handkerchief belonging to his wife seen in Cassio's hand was enough for the deluded Othello to pass sentence of death upon them both, without once questioning how Cassio came by it. Desdemona had never given such a present to Cassio, nor would she have wronged her lord by doing anything so nasty as giving his presents to another man. Both Cassio and Desdemona were innocent, but the wicked Iago had made his wife, a good but a weak woman, steal this handkerchief from Desdemona by pretending she wanted to copy the embroidery. In reality, Iago had dropped it near Cassio, where he might find it.

Soon after meeting his wife, Othello pretended to have a headache and asked her to lend him her handkerchief to hold to his temples. She did so. 'Not this one,' Othello said, 'but the handkerchief I gave you.' Desdemona, of course, didn't have it, for it had been stolen. Othello said, 'This is a fault indeed. An Egyptian woman gave that handkerchief to my mother. The woman was a witch and could read people's thoughts. She told my mother that it would make her good-natured and my father would love her but if she lost it or gave it away, my father's feelings would turn and he would loathe her as much as he had loved her. When she was dying she gave it me and asked me, if I ever married, to give it to my wife. I did so. Take care of it. Make it as precious as your own eye.'

'Is it possible?' said the frightened lady.

'It is true,' Othello continued. 'It is a magical handkerchief. A fortune-teller, who lived two hundred years, embroidered it in a fit of prophetic fury. The silkworms that produced the silk were holy and it was coloured with magical dye.'

Desdemona, hearing about the amazing power of the handkerchief, was ready to die with fear, for she plainly realized that she had lost it and with it, she feared, the love of her husband.

Othello looked strange and angry and kept on asking for the handkerchief, which she could not produce. She tried to divert her husband from such serious thoughts and cheerfully told him she saw all his talk about the handkerchief was only to put her off from her request for Michael Cassio. She went on to praise him, just as Iago had foretold, till Othello in total distraction burst out of the room. Then Desdemona, though unwillingly, began to suspect her lord was jealous.

She had no idea how she could have made him jealous and then she accused herself for accusing him. He was probably disturbed by some unexpected news from Venice or some state troubles. She said, 'Men are not gods and we cannot expect them to be as loving and thoughtful once they are married as they were on the wedding day.' She told herself off for so unkindly judging his unkindness.

Again Othello and Desdemona met and he accused her more plainly of being unfaithful and of loving another man, but he did not name whom. Othello cried and Desdemona said, 'This is dreadful, why are you crying?' Othello told her that he could bravely have put up with all sorts of evils — poverty, disease and disgrace — but her unfaithfulness had broken his heart. He wished she had never been born. When he had

gone, this innocent lady was so dazed at her lord's untrue suspicion of her that she felt exhausted. She asked her attendant to make her bed and to lay her wedding sheets upon it, saying that when people teach children, they do it by gentle means and easy tasks. Othello might have treated her like this, for she was but a child when she was told off. This was all the complaint which this gentle lady made.

Desdemona expected her husband to follow her to bed and soon fell asleep. When Othello came in, he was full of the wicked purpose which he had planned of putting his lady to death. When he saw her asleep, he thought he could not shed her blood, nor scar her beautiful white skin, but he was determined that she should die. Otherwise, as he said, she would live to betray more men as she had him. Then he kissed her for the last time, but that kiss was so sweet he had to kiss her again. He cried, but he said they were cruel tears.

Desdemona was woken by his kisses and she looked at Othello. She saw him bite his lips and roll his eyes and she knew that he was always unchanging when he looked like that. He told her to prepare for death and to say her prayers, for he would not kill her soul. This innocent wife, as she lay at his mercy, begged for pity and to be told her fault. Then he named Cassio and mentioned the handkerchief which, he said, she had given him. As she tried to clear herself, he suddenly would hear no more, but covering her up in the bedclothes, stifled her to death.

At this same time, Cassio, wounded and bleeding, was brought into the house. Iago had set one of his people to kill Cassio, but the man had failed. Cassio was wounded, but not fatally. Iago killed the other man to prevent discovery, but letters found in his pockets made Iago's guilt and Cassio's innocence clear beyond all doubt. Cassio now came to beg pardon of Othello and to ask what he had done to make him employ Iago to murder him.

This discovery was like a thunderbolt to Othello, who now plainly saw that he was no better than a murderer and his wife, poor innocent lady, had always been faithful to him. The awfulness of this discovery made his life unbearable. He fell upon his sword and throwing himself upon the body of his dear mistreated lady, died.

These terrible actions aroused feelings of horror and amazement in the bystanders, for Othello had always been a good man and, till he was worked on by the cunning of Iago, he was a loving and adoring husband. He had loved not wisely, but too well and his manly eyes, when he learned his mistake, though not used to crying, had dropped tears as fast as Arabian trees drop their gum. When he was dead, all his former merits and his brave acts were remembered. Nothing now was left to be done but to put the strictest law in force against Iago and to send word to Venice of the sad death of their famous general.

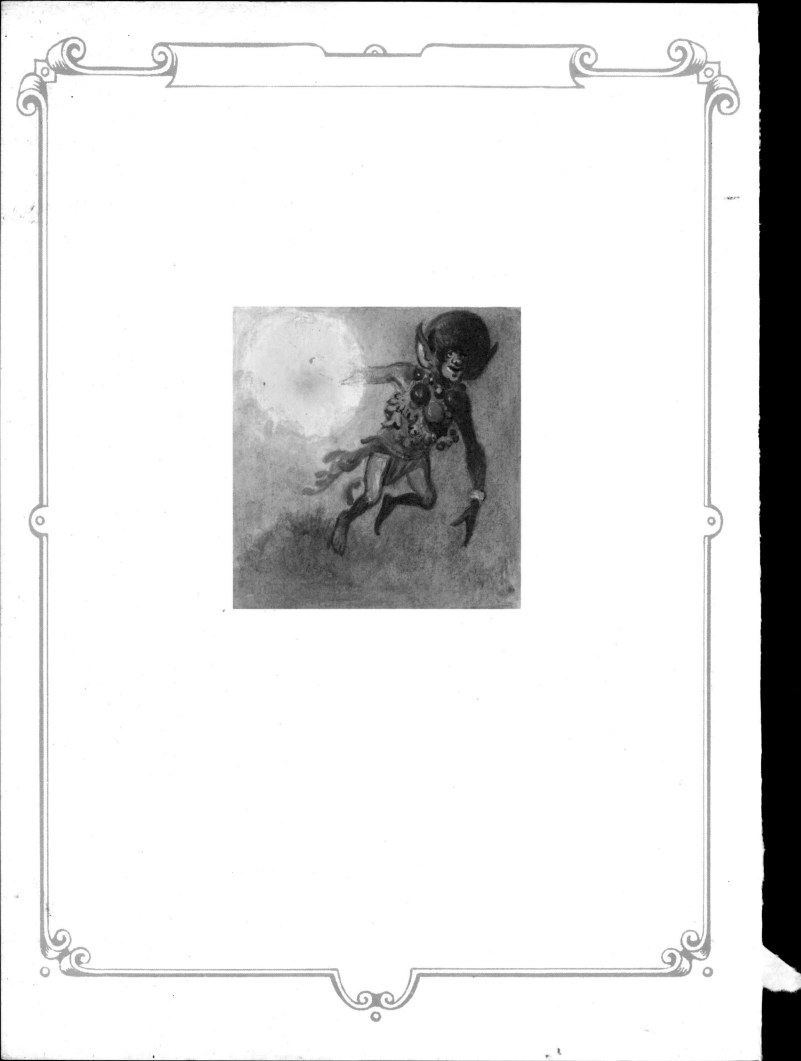